"Why did you marry me, David?" Christy said.

"I married you because I've always loved you."

Joy bubbled up inside Christy. "That's wonderful."

"Wonderful? What's so wonderful about it? It just makes everything more complicated."

"No, it doesn't. It makes it simpler."

David shook his head slowly. "Loving each other doesn't change anything."

He was wrong. The fact that he loved her changed everything. "You just wait," she said. "After a year, you're not going to be able to let me go."

Books by Cynthia Rutledge

Love Inspired

Unforgettable Faith #102
Undercover Angel #123
The Marrying Kind #135
Redeeming Claire #151
Judging Sara #157
Wedding Bell Blues #178

Silhouette Romance

Trish's Not-So-Little Secret #1581

CYNTHIA RUTLEDGE

enjoys making the characters in her head come to life and visiting the places that they live. To research *Wedding Bell Blues,* Cynthia and her husband took a trip to Las Vegas and in three short days saw the inside of a dozen wedding chapels and more than a few casinos. Though not much of a gambler—she can't even win when the odds are 50-50—she feels she hit the jackpot when she sold her first book in 1999. And her lucky streak has continued. *Wedding Bell Blues* is her sixth book for the Love Inspired line. She also writes for Silhouette Romance.

Cynthia encourages readers to visit her Web site at http://www.cynthiarutledge.com.

Wedding Bell Blues
Cynthia Rutledge

Love Inspired®

Published by Steeple Hill Books™

STEEPLE HILL BOOKS

ISBN 0-373-87185-6

WEDDING BELL BLUES

Copyright © 2002 by Cynthia Rutledge

All rights reserved. Except for use in any review, the reproduction or utilization of this work in whole or in part in any form by any electronic, mechanical or other means, now known or hereafter invented, including xerography, photocopying and recording, or in any information storage or retrieval system, is forbidden without the written permission of the editorial office, Steeple Hill Books, 300 East 42nd Street, New York, NY 10017 U.S.A.

All characters in this book have no existence outside the imagination of the author and have no relation whatsoever to anyone bearing the same name or names. They are not even distantly inspired by any individual known or unknown to the author, and all incidents are pure invention.

This edition published by arrangement with Steeple Hill Books.

® and TM are trademarks of Steeple Hill Books, used under license. Trademarks indicated with ® are registered in the United States Patent and Trademark Office, the Canadian Trade Marks Office and in other countries.

Visit us at www.steeplehill.com

Printed in U.S.A.

...I will be with you:
I will never leave you nor forsake you.
—*Joshua* 1:5

To Wendy, my daughter and best friend.

Chapter One

Christy Fairchild could have sworn Elvis winked at her.

One minute the paunchy king of rock 'n' roll, resplendent in a white jumpsuit, was pronouncing her and David Warner married, the next he was giving her a knowing smile as she and her new husband were hustled aside to make room for the next couple.

"You two are lucky we had a cancellation." The shapely assistant with the bouffant hairstyle and overdone makeup à la early Priscilla Presley smiled and handed them their wedding pictures. "Most chapels in Las Vegas are booked a year in advance for Valentine's Day."

"It was a last-minute kind of thing," Christy

murmured as she took the photos, the huge marquis diamond on her finger twinkling in the light. She stared down at the ring.

"Regrets?" Her new husband's voice was warm against her ear.

It had been six months since she'd had a real date and a lifetime since David had been a part of her life. But tonight, on the spur of the moment, she'd scrapped her plans to do a little shopping and instead married a man she hadn't seen in ten years.

"Not a one," she said, smiling up at him. It surprised her that she actually meant the words. Normally she was a worrier, second-guessing every decision and analyzing everything to death. The combination of the antihistamine she'd taken earlier and the glass of wine she'd had in the lounge with David must have affected her more than she'd realized.

"Chrissy." His voice was deep and low. He was the only one she'd ever known who called her by that name. "Do you want to go back to your place or mine?"

Christy looked up and met his gaze. A shiver of anticipation traveled up her spine.

They were married. It had been her dream when she was seventeen. Now it had come true.

Had she ever known a more handsome man? His broad shoulders filled out his dinner jacket to perfection and his dark hair gleamed in the fluorescent glare. But it was his eyes that captivated her. They were hazel, but could change to gold or green depending on his mood or the clothes he wore. Right now there was a curious intensity in their golden depths that was as unsettling as it was exciting.

"Did anyone ever tell you that you have beautiful eyes?" Christy reached up and ran the tip of her finger along his jawline. "Or that you're irresistible when you smile?"

A forgotten dimple flashed in his cheek. "So does that mean you won't be able to tell me no? No matter what I ask?"

"Right now I'd say—" her voice sounded husky even to her own ears "—your wish is pretty much my command. Tell me what you have in mind."

His eyes darkened and he opened his mouth as if to speak, but he never got the chance. Before he could answer Christy wrapped her arms around his neck and kissed him, deciding it might be best if she showed him first what *she* had in mind.

Christy's lips curved into a smile even before she opened her eyes. What a beautiful dream it had been. She and David Warner toasting each other with champagne in the Jacuzzi, kissing on the balcony, making love in her king-size bed…

Her eyes popped open and her breath caught in her throat. The smell of his cologne, the taste of his lips, the feel of his hands on her skin was so vivid, so graphic she could almost believe it had been real.

But how could that be? She'd never been with a man before, not in that way. A warmth stole up her neck.

It must have been the whole Valentine's Day thing, she decided. Since she'd never been in Las Vegas before, staying over after her seminar ended had seemed like a good idea at the time. Unfortunately she'd been unprepared for the hype that went along with this day for lovers. That explained why the wedding chapel had been in her dreams. And David Warner? That wasn't hard to figure out. Her best Valentine's Day celebration had been with him her senior year in high school.

Christy smiled wryly. Dreaming of wedding chapels and an old boyfriend had to be a sign of a seriously deficient social life. She was going to have to get out more.

Though even if she did find time to start dating again it'd be a long time before she'd be standing in any wedding chapel saying her vows. Marriage for her was a lifetime commitment and she wasn't going to marry any man until she knew he was the one God intended her to be with forever.

No wonder her subconscious had brought up David Warner. At one time she'd been convinced he was her "forever love." When he'd asked for his ring back right before high school graduation, she'd thought her heart would crack in two. But their breakup was the best thing that could have happened. They'd been totally wrong for each other. She realized that now.

She shook her head. Thank goodness she'd outgrown that youthful foolishness. Wisdom now tempered her actions, and consequently her life ran like clockwork. Staying over an extra day in Las Vegas had been an impulsive move, but after six months on the road she thought she'd earned a break.

Today she'd be back on schedule. She'd check out of the hotel, grab a plane back to Chicago and be in her apartment in Lincoln Park before dinner. Though she didn't have to present her ideas regarding the next series of seminars to her manager for a couple of weeks, Christy wanted to get a jump start. Order brought calm to her life. She didn't like being late and she didn't like rushing. That's why she'd be at the airport well ahead of her ten-o'clock flight.

Rolling to her side, she glanced at her travel clock. She took a second look. Nine-thirty?

Christy bolted upright and the bedcovers

dropped to her waist. The moment they did Christy became conscious of cold air hitting her bare skin.

Bare skin?

Christy dropped her gaze. Her eyes widened. Where were her cotton pajamas? Though many people slept in the nude, she never had.

"Christy?"

Her head jerked up and her mouth dropped open.

David Warner stood in the bathroom doorway wearing only a towel wrapped around his waist. Still damp, his hair spiked up, while the dark strands on his chest glistened with drops of water.

She blinked once.

He didn't disappear.

She blinked again.

He shifted from one foot to the other and stared, a strange look in his eyes. Her heart pounded in her chest. He was real. Standing in her hotel room. Looking even more incredible at twenty-eight than he had at eighteen.

Christy gasped, suddenly realizing where his gaze was focused. With one swift yank she pulled the bedspread up to her neck, wishing with all her heart that she could pull it over her head.

Instead, she lifted her chin and ignored the rapid beating of her heart and the heat burning her cheeks. "What are you doing in my room?"

If he'd noticed the curtness in her tone, it didn't show. His gaze searched hers. "I think you know the answer to that."

A shiver traveled up her spine and her sense of unease skyrocketed.

It couldn't be true. It was just part of the nightmare.

"We met in the lobby?" he prompted, taking a seat on the edge of the bed. "You said you were in Vegas because of some seminar. I was here because of my grandfather's birthday."

It had been part of the dream, the chance meeting by the front desk, the decision to stop in the lounge for a drink to catch up on old times.

"You were supposed to go to the Wayne Newton show at the Stardust," she said slowly, keeping her gaze focused on his face and trying to ignore his broad shoulders and muscular chest.

He nodded, his expression inscrutable. "But we got to talking and one thing led to another."

One thing led to another.

Christy tried to still her rising panic. She'd been tired and hadn't had much to eat for dinner but still, she couldn't have had more than a drink or two. Besides, there wasn't enough alcohol in the world to make her abandon her moral values and go to bed with a man she hadn't seen in ten years. Still, the evidence seemed overwhelming.

"You spent the night," she said, surprised she could sound so calm. "You and I made love."

She said it as a statement of fact, hoping he'd tell her no. Instead he nodded.

"You do remember." He studied her face with his enigmatic gaze for an extra beat.

Her chest tightened and it was all Christy could do not to break down and cry. She'd always tried to follow a Godly path. How could she have gotten so off course? This man she barely knew had held her, kissed her, caressed her. And not only had she let him, she had the feeling she'd encouraged him.

"This may not mean anything to you." She took a deep breath and wondered why she was even bothering to explain. "But I always vowed that the only man I'd ever sleep with would be my husband."

David's tense expression softened. He reached over and took her left hand, lifting it so she could see the ring.

"You didn't break that vow, Christy," he said quietly. "You and I were married last night."

Chapter Two

The room spun like an out-of-control tilt-a-whirl and Christy swallowed hard against the bile rising in her throat. "You're lying," she said wildly, even though she knew it was the truth. "It was only a dream. I wouldn't have married you. We're all wrong for each other."

"That may well be." The muscle in his jaw twitched but his expression remained carefully controlled. "But the fact remains we are married. Now we have to decide what we're going to do about it."

"What do you mean?" she said.

His expression darkened with an unreadable emotion. "We could get an annulment."

Annulment.

Did he really think a few strokes of a pen could obliterate the night they'd spent together? Heat filled her cheeks. Even now her pulses skittered alarmingly at the memory and there was a tingling in the pit of her stomach.

"I think you've forgotten one important fact." Christy cleared her throat. "The marriage has been consummated."

She tried to speak calmly, hoping that if they kept their emotions out of this, they might be able to come to a sane, rational solution. Even though at this point Christy wasn't sure exactly what that would be. "I guess what I'm trying to say is, it's a little late for an annulment."

"All right, then, a divorce?" He lifted a dark brow, his voice filled with as much emotion as one would use to order room service.

I'll have two eggs poached, some whole wheat toast and a divorce on the side.

Divorce.

Just the word made her shudder. For the past four years of her life she'd built a name for herself, traveling coast-to-coast lecturing on the institution of marriage, on ways to make bad marriages better and good marriages stronger. Ways to ensure that a couple stayed together forever.

But now she'd entered into that sacred institution in haste. Would she be the next one getting a divorce? Breaking a promise made before God and man because it was an easy way out of a difficult situation?

But was the easiest way the right way?

Christy took a deep breath and briefly closed her eyes.

Dear God, I've made such a mess of my life. I thought I had all the answers—now all I have are questions. Please tell me what I should do.

When she opened her eyes David was watching her intently, still waiting for a response. She wished she knew what he was thinking. Did he want her to agree with him? Or would he be willing to do the unthinkable and give their marriage a chance?

"David." Christy's voice trembled with emotion. She took a deep breath and tried again. "Divorce may seem to be a ready solution to our problem. But—"

A knock sounded at the door. Christy swung a panicked gaze to David.

"Get on some clothes," she hissed.

"It's probably just housekeeping," he said, reaching for the shirt and pants he'd worn last night. But when his hand moved to the towel around his waist, Christy averted her gaze.

"Could you come back later?" she called to the closed door. "I won't be checking out quite yet."

"Miss Fairchild," a deep voice answered. "I'm Andrew Lowell and I'm a reporter with the *Las Vegas Review-Journal*. I apologize for interrupting your honeymoon, but I'd like to ask you a few questions about your marriage last night."

"So much for keeping things quiet," she muttered.

Now that the local press had the news, it wouldn't be long before the wire services picked it up. Her heart sank to her feet.

Though Christy had no intention of letting the reporter in, she couldn't let him go without finding out what he knew. She wrapped the sheet around her like a toga and hobbled across the room.

"Mr. Lowell, answer a question for me. How did you find out about my marriage?"

"Miss Fairchild, nothing that goes on in this town's wedding chapels stays a secret for long." The man's laughter echoed through the door. "Especially when a noted authority on keeping marriages together takes the plunge herself. I really would appreciate five minutes of your time."

It seemed incredibly rude to be talking through a closed door, but Christy had been around her share of reporters. She knew if she opened the door even a crack, she might find herself on the front page of some tabloid dressed only in a sheet.

"I'm afraid now is not a good time, Mr. Lowell.

But if you'll slip your name under the door, my publicist will be in touch.''

''But, Ms. Fairchild—''

''Goodbye, Mr. Lowell.'' Christy turned her back to the door and faced David.

''Looks like a quick divorce is out of the question now,'' David said, buttoning his cuffs.

Her heart tightened in her chest. For their marriage to stand a chance, they would both have to decide to make it work. She couldn't do it alone.

She stared at David for a long moment and wondered what he would say if she told him she wanted to see if they could beat the odds. Would he be willing to back such a long shot? Could she convince him to go for broke and try to make their made-in-Vegas vows work?

David tossed Christy's room key onto the desk in his room and sank into a nearby chair. After making sure the reporter had gone, he'd made his getaway, leaving Christy to shower and get dressed. Over breakfast they would discuss their future.

Married.

It hardly seemed possible. Granted, he'd expected to come back from Las Vegas engaged. But it was his longtime friend Lauren Carlyle who he'd thought would be wearing his ring.

After all, he was pushing thirty and he needed a wife. His grandfather's dictate had made that clear. Marrying for love just didn't seem to be in the cards. But he and Lauren were good friends. They both wanted the same things out of life—a home, a couple of kids and time to spend with family and friends. She said she loved him. He'd hoped that one day he'd love her, too.

When he'd seen a marquis diamond advertised as part of a "take a chance on romance" promotion, David had taken it as a sign. He'd pop the question and give Lauren the ring during the Las Vegas trip.

But instead, the diamond had ended up on Christy's hand. One minute they were sitting in the lounge laughing about his need for a wife and her need for a husband and the next thing he knew they were flipping a coin—heads they married, tails they walked away. It had started out as a joke. Now the joke was on him.

He'd married a woman just like his mother. A woman so focused on her career that her family would always come second. A woman who could never give him the kind of home life he craved.

He would have asked himself how it had happened, but David already knew the answer. Whenever he and Christy got together electricity sizzled in the air. They were like two magnets fighting to keep a distance but drawn to each other by an unseen force.

David raked his fingers through his hair. He'd had more sense when he was eighteen. At least then he'd walked away from her. Now, thanks to one reckless impulse, she was his wife. For the moment, anyway.

"I know it seemed like a good idea at the time." Christy sat back against the vinyl seat of the restaurant booth and pushed the food around the plate with a fork. "But right now I haven't a clue what we were thinking."

"Didn't you tell me your publicist thought being married would be a big boost to your career?" David gazed at her over the top of his coffee cup.

Christy frowned at his emphasis on the word *career*. He made it sound like a dirty word. "That's true, but I'd told him I wasn't going to marry just to get better tour sponsors."

She could tell by the look in his eyes that he didn't believe her, but she didn't waste her breath trying to convince him.

David set his cup on the table and folded his hands. "Knowing the chemistry between us, if I had it to do over again, when I saw you in that lobby I'd have walked the other way. I'm guessing you'd do the same."

Christy slowly nodded. She wished she'd never set eyes on David Warner. Or that wedding chapel.

"But what's done is done," David said. "The only question that matters is, where do we go from here?"

The same doubts and fears that she could hear in his voice were fluttering like a thousand crazy butterflies in her stomach. She didn't want to be married any more than he did, but she didn't want to make a second mistake by rushing into divorce, either. "We could try to make it work?"

David stared at his coffee cup for a long moment before heaving a resigned sigh. "The way I look at it, if we split now, not only will your career suffer but I'll lose my chance to take over Warner Enterprises. Granddad won't sign the company over until I've been married a year. So we don't have much choice except *to* stay together."

"I have to agree with you," Christy said. Her analytical side appreciated his straightforward, no-nonsense approach. But the romantic part of her wished he'd tempered what he'd said with a few sweet words of reassurance. She shoved the regret aside. "What happens now?"

"I suggest we take it a step at a time," he said. "The first step is for you to get reacquainted with my family. You can do that over dinner tonight."

"Tonight?" Christy's voice, normally rich and full, came out in a high-pitched squeak.

"They have to find out sometime." David lifted the cup of coffee to his lips and took a sip.

"Any thoughts on how we're going to explain this sudden marriage?" She lifted a brow and tried to mimic his cool composure.

"Leave that to me," David said. "I'll think of something."

"You'd better come up with something quick," Christy said. "I've never been good at 'winging it.'"

She brushed back a strand of hair with a shaky hand. Her life was spiraling out of control and she couldn't seem to stop the nosedive.

As if he could read her thoughts, David's expression softened. "It will be okay. I promise."

He leaned across the table and took her hand, touching her for the first time since they'd made love.

Christy shivered. She wanted to pull away, but she couldn't make herself break the contact.

A smile tipped David's lips and he gently turned her hand over, massaging her palm with his thumb. A languid warmth filled her limbs and Christy suddenly realized that her response to this man had nothing to do with reason and everything to do with how he made her feel.

He looked up and met her gaze. His eyes darkened. Without saying a word, David brought her hand to his lips.

Her heart picked up speed.

"Christy Fairchild?" a feminine voice shrieked in her ear. "Is that you?"

Christy jerked back.

A tall woman in a purple jogging suit stood beside the table. Everything about the woman was angular—from her long pointy nails to her stiletto sandals. Even her chin veered to a V. But her smile was contagious, and once Christy's heart slowed to a regular rhythm she couldn't help but smile back.

"I'm Alice Hudkins," the woman said.

Christy lifted her shoulders in a helpless shrug.

"I was in your 'Together Forever' workshop at the convention center," Alice said. "I was the one who asked the question about trial separations."

"Of course." The fog cleared for a moment and Christy had a vague recollection of a woman in fuchsia frantically waving her hand. "I remember now. You were seated to the left of the stage."

"That's right." The woman smiled in relief.

"I'm glad you stopped by," Christy said.

At any other time Christy would have enjoyed visiting with one of her fans. But now, though she tried to be cordial, she hoped the woman would get the hint that she and David wanted to be left alone.

"Aren't you going to introduce me to your friend?" Bright with curiosity, the woman's gaze shifted to David.

Christy groaned to herself. Alice clearly wasn't going to fade away. At least, not until she'd gotten her introduction. Should Christy take the big step and make it official or pass David off as just a friend?

The man at her side had no such qualms.

"David Warner." He stood and extended his hand, flashing the woman a dazzling smile. "Christy's husband."

"You're married?" The woman's smile widened.

Christy swallowed hard and nodded. "As of last night."

"I knew it," the woman said triumphantly. "I told my sister that there was something special between you two."

David's dimple flashed.

Alice giggled like a giddy schoolgirl. "You seemed so calm at the seminar. I can't believe you had a wedding in the works. And I can't believe you didn't tell us."

Though her words were directed to Christy, her gaze remained on David.

"Christy wanted to say something at the seminar, but I thought it would be more romantic if it was our little secret.'' David leaned over and took Christy's hand again, lifting it to his lips. ''Don't you agree?''

Christy found herself nodding along with Alice. Her hand tingled, and though she knew it was all for show, she couldn't keep her lips from curving in a silly grin.

Alice sighed heavily. ''It's incredibly romantic.''

''Would you like to join us?'' David asked ''Christy and I—''

''Thank you for the kind invitation, Mr. Warner. But this is your honeymoon,'' Alice said, with a hint of regret in her gaze. ''You certainly don't need to be spending it gabbing with an old woman.''

David started to protest, but the woman shook her head, her expression wistful. ''Love is such a special gift from God. I hope you both realize how lucky you are.''

Lucky?

Christy slanted a sideways glance at David. Right now she'd give anything to be so lucky. Not the seven-come-eleven kind of lucky. Or the megawinner-slot machine kind of lucky. All she wanted was to be a woman lucky enough to be in love with the man she married. And even more important, lucky enough to be loved back.

Chapter Three

Christy took one last look in the mirror. Her blond hair fell in loose curls to her shoulders and she'd taken extra care with her makeup. Though she looked perfectly presentable in her black linen sheath, she couldn't help but worry.

What would David's family think when they heard the news? After all, anyone with an ounce of sense had to wonder what kind of woman would marry a man she hadn't seen in ten years.

Desperate was the word that came to her mind. But in Christy's case that didn't apply. Though her publicist *had* told her she'd go further in her career if she were married, she'd known what she wanted in a husband and she'd been determined to wait for the right man—forever if necessary.

An image of David's handsome face flashed before her, and though Christy had to concede a man couldn't get much better looking than David Warner, looks had never been at the top of her list.

Still, he *had* looked oh-so-handsome when she'd first set eyes on him in the lobby. And he'd looked even better when he'd taken off his jacket and tie. And when he'd...

Christy reined in her thoughts and reminded herself there was a lot more to a successful marriage than physical attraction. Unfortunately, at this time, she and David had little else to go on.

She dabbed on a little lip gloss, snapped her purse shut and glanced around the room. The bellhop should be here any time to transfer her bags to David's room. Their life together was about to begin and never had she felt so unprepared.

Several brisk raps against the door pulled her from her reverie.

"Christy? Are you ready?"

She wiped her suddenly damp palms on her dress. "Coming."

On her way to the door Christy pushed in a half-open drawer and shut off the bathroom light, finding comfort in familiar actions. Unlatching the chain, she slowly opened the door and stepped into the hall.

"Wow." David stepped back. Though he was

ten minutes late, he didn't hurry. His gaze lingered and a look of approval filled his eyes. "You are so incredibly beautiful."

Christy couldn't stem the pleasure that flowed through her at his words. "You're looking pretty good yourself."

Good was an understatement. David's charcoal pants and light-gray shirt and tie were stylishly elegant and he wore them with an easy self-assurance that was infinitely appealing. And it didn't hurt that he smelled as good as he looked. Christy breathed in the scent that had permeated her dreams, and her heart picked up speed. Her gaze rose to meet his.

His eyes darkened. "You are so lovely."

"I think you said that before," she protested halfheartedly, knowing he could say it a hundred times and it wouldn't be too much.

A slight smile lifted his lips and David raised one hand, lightly touching her cheek.

Her skin prickled and turned to gooseflesh.

David moved closer, and Christy closed her eyes. Every fiber of her body anticipated his kiss.

He lowered his lips.

She held her breath.

A door slammed down the hall and the sound of laughter filled the corridor.

Christy took a step back, her heart pounding in her chest.

David exhaled a harsh breath, and when she met his gaze Christy knew the disappointment in his eyes mirrored her own. "We'd better get going."

"I guess so," Christy said reluctantly.

The boisterous group from down the hall joined them on the elevator ride to the main floor. It wasn't until she and David had gotten off and were halfway across the casino floor that Christy realized she had no idea what David planned to say to his family.

She grabbed his arm and pulled him to a stop. "I'm not sure this is the right thing to do."

"You said you wanted to play this out." His gaze narrowed. "Have you changed your mind?"

"No, not at all." Christy shifted her gaze to the flashing lights of a nearby slot machine and took a deep breath. David had completely misunderstood her. She wanted to see his family again, she really did. But why did it have to be tonight? She and David had barely had a chance to talk, much less get their stories straight. "I'm just nervous about going into this meeting so unprepared."

"It's a dinner, not a meeting." His fingers tipped her chin to meet his gaze. "And I'm nervous, too. But remember what we decided? We're taking it a step at a time. Tonight is the first step."

It had made sense when they'd talked about it. But Christy had always been a planner. The concept of taking something day by day was as foreign to her as taking a vacation on the spur of the moment. Unfortunately she didn't have much choice in this situation.

"You're right." Christy smiled with more confidence than she felt. "I don't know why I'm so stressed. After all, I've met your grandfather and cousin before."

"And you know Lauren," David said, as if that should make her feel better and not worse.

Lauren. The woman he'd dated off and on for years. The woman he'd intended to propose to in Las Vegas. The woman who in high school had been Christy's best friend.

Christy cleared her throat. "I didn't think Lauren would be joining us."

"Why wouldn't she?" David's surprise showed in his voice. "She didn't know I was going to ask her to marry me. As far as she's concerned, we're just friends."

Though David had continued to insist that there had been no real talk of commitment between him and Lauren, Christy had her doubts. The fact that Lauren had been invited to come to Las Vegas to help celebrate his grandfather's eightieth birthday seemed to indicate otherwise. "I wouldn't want her to feel uncomfortable."

"You let me worry about that," David said, taking her arm. "We'd better get going. I don't want to keep them waiting."

Christy glanced at her watch and picked up the pace. David was right. If they didn't hurry, they *were* going to be late. And she certainly didn't want the evening to start off on a sour note.

They got a taxi right away, but the traffic moved at a snail's pace along the strip. By the time they reached their destination—a French café inside the Paris Hotel complex—the hostess told them that their party had already been seated. David's hand rested lightly against Christy's back as they wove their way through the linen-clad tables toward the back of the restaurant.

She spotted David's grandfather first. Though the man was eighty, he still retained a commanding presence. A distinguished-looking gentleman with a shock of white hair, he sat at the head of the table with all the presence of a CEO presiding over a board of directors meeting. On his right sat David's cousin, Blake.

Even as a boy Blake had never been as handsome or athletic as David. Now, ten years later, the difference was even more pronounced. Blake's hair had thinned and his face had a fleshy softness that spoke of too much fine dining and too little exercise. She didn't recognize the woman sitting beside him. Christy decided she must be his wife.

That left the brunette with her back to them. *Lauren.* And next to Lauren was one empty chair.

Christy's feet slowed, but David's hand pushed her forward.

"Sorry we kept you waiting." David started to pull out the chair, then stopped, only then realizing what Christy had already noticed.

An uneasy feeling traveled up her spine. She'd assumed David had told his family they were married and that this was going to be a "getting to know you" kind of dinner. Now she wasn't so sure.

"I told you I was bringing Christy." David motioned impatiently for the waiter to bring another chair.

"No, you just said you had a surprise." His grandfather rose and smiled at Christy. "I believe I know this young lady, although I'm afraid I've forgotten your last name."

"Fairchild," she said automatically. The fact that she was legally a Warner still hadn't sunk in. "I don't blame you for not remembering, Mr. Warner. It's been a long time and we only met one time. It was a Christmas Eve service. David and I sat with you and your wife."

"That's right. I remember now." The older man nodded. "I'm sorry to say that Myra is no longer with us. She passed on three years ago."

"I'm so sorry," Christy murmured.

A look of sadness crossed the older man's face. "I attend services alone now. David doesn't seem to be interested in going to church."

The older gentleman's tone told Christy what he thought of that behavior.

Blake stifled a smile.

David's jaw tightened.

An uneasy silence descended over the group.

"It's been a few years since chemistry." Blake broke the silence and offered Christy an engaging grin. "Hopefully you haven't forgotten those fun-filled days."

"I remember." How could she forget? She'd been convinced that having Blake as her lab partner had been part of some diabolical plan to drive her crazy. Blake had been convinced he was God's gift to women. He'd asked her out repeatedly. But his persistence hadn't bothered her half as much as the fact that he'd pursued her knowing she was his cousin's girlfriend. "And this must be your wife?"

"I'm Karen." The woman's smile was warm and welcoming. "It's nice to meet you."

"Nice to meet you, too." Christy shifted her

gaze to the silent brunette. "Hello, Lauren. It's been a long time."

Lauren flashed Christy a smile that looked so phony, Christy wondered why she'd even bothered. "You're right, it—"

"Enough of the chitchat." David's grandfather waved a silencing hand. "We know Christy, she knows us. Now, let's get down to business."

"Get down to business?" David waited until Christy had sat down before pulling up the extra chair the waiter had brought.

"I think I speak for all of us when I say we're anxious to hear your surprise." His grandfather quirked a snow-white brow. "We can't wait to find out what could have been so important that it would make you give up front-row tickets to Wayne."

David had told Christy his grandfather was a big Wayne Newton fan and that's why the man had chosen to celebrate his eightieth birthday in Las Vegas. But Christy knew the hurt in the older man's eyes was more about his grandson missing his birthday celebration than his missing an opportunity to see Mr. Las Vegas.

David paused and Christy offered him an encouraging smile. She was glad it was him and not her who had to find the right words to mend the hurt feelings.

"Granddad, let me start by saying I'm sorry I missed your party. I really am."

The tense lines on the older man's face relaxed a little at the sincerity in his grandson's voice. But David wasn't out of the woods yet. He'd offered an apology, not an explanation.

The older man shifted his gaze to Christy. "I have the feeling that Miss Fairchild had something to do with your no-show last night. Am I right?"

Christy just smiled.

"As a matter of fact, she did." David draped his arm across the back of Christy's chair and met his grandfather's gaze. "I was on my way to the Stardust when I ran into Christy. We started talking and decided to have a glass of wine in the lounge. Catch up on old times. One thing led to another—"

"Goodness, David. Your grandfather wasn't asking for a complete rundown of your night's activities," Lauren interrupted with a nervous laugh. "What he was trying to say is that we were worried. It was his birthday and you were nowhere to be found. When we called your room and you weren't there, we even thought about calling the police. Where were you, anyway?"

"I was in Christy's room," David said abruptly. "I spent the night."

"David!" Lauren's eyes widened.

"Son, this isn't appropriate for—"

"Granddad, it's okay." David met his grandfather's gaze. "Christy and I were married last night."

So much for finding just the right words.

Christy clasped her hands in her lap, lifted her chin and forced a bright smile.

For an instant Lauren's face blanched. Then her green eyes flashed. "That's really not funny, David."

"It's no joke." His arm tightened around Christy's shoulders. "We got a license, found a wedding chapel that had a cancellation, and got married."

"You're serious." Blake's gaze shifted from David to Christy.

David nodded.

"Well, I'd say congratulations are definitely in order," David's grandfather said without missing a beat. Though clearly stunned, the older man responded with surprising aplomb. He leaned across the table to shake David's hand while flashing Christy a warm smile.

"Congratulations?" Lauren's shrill voice cut the air like a knife and several people at a nearby table turned to stare. "He marries a woman he hasn't seen since high school and you congratulate him? On what? His stupidity?"

Karen gasped.

Blake settled back in his chair and crossed his arms, his bemused gaze shifting from Christy to his cousin.

David's hand clenched into a fist behind Christy's back and she could feel the tension emanating from him.

"You were dating *me*," Lauren said, shooting Christy a piercing glare. "Now you up and marry this—"

"Lauren, what's done is done." Though David's grandfather's voice was soft and low, his tone brooked no argument. "David and Christy go way back. I don't know the whole story about what happened last night, but I do know that sometimes those old feelings never die."

"David broke up with her in high school. He hasn't seen her in years." Lauren turned to David. "Were you drunk? Is that what happened? I know you don't normally drink, but that's the only explanation that makes any sense."

Lauren's response shouldn't have surprised Christy, but it did. She could feel David tense beside her.

"I married Christy because I love her." David's voice resonated with a steely-edged control. "I've loved her since high school."

Though Christy didn't believe him for a second,

she had to admit his words sounded sincere. And she marveled at how easily the lie slid from his lips.

Lauren's gaze shifted from David to Christy, her look clearly disbelieving.

"We're very happy for both of you." Karen's sweet voice filled the silence. "Aren't we, honey?"

Blake hesitated, then nodded. "Very happy."

"I'm not going to be able to stay for dinner after all." In one fluid movement Lauren grabbed her purse and shoved back her chair. Without another word, she headed toward the door.

Though the woman hadn't been her friend in years, they'd once been close and Christy could feel her pain.

"Go and talk to her, David," Christy said softly, keeping her voice so low only he could hear. "You owe her that much."

David hesitated for only a second before rising. "I'll be right back."

Christy's gaze followed him until he was out of sight. When she turned back, she found three pairs of curious eyes fixed upon her. Smiling brightly, she picked up the menu and glanced around the table. "Are we ready to order yet? I'm starving."

"Lauren, wait." David finally caught up with her on the sidewalk in front of the hotel. Grabbing her arm, he pulled her off to the side. "We need to talk."

"Don't you think it's a little late for that?" Her gaze dropped to his hand gripping her arm.

He released his hold. "Lauren, cut me some slack. We've been friends too long to let this come between us."

She tilted her head and stared at him for a long moment. "You don't get it, do you? You're married. We can't be friends. We can't be anything anymore."

Two tears slipped down her cheeks. She hurriedly brushed them away with the back of her hand.

David's heart twisted. He liked Lauren. His grandfather used to say they were like two peas in a pod. They had the same likes and dislikes, they ran in the same social circle. They had been friends for years.

Though he'd never been physically attracted to Lauren, he cared for her. And he knew she would have been a good wife to him.

He drew a ragged breath.

"Why did you marry her, David?" Lauren's sad gaze lingered on his face. "And don't tell me you love her, because I know you don't."

Of course he didn't love Christy. He barely

knew her. But she was his wife, at least for now. He owed her his loyalty.

Lauren took his hand in hers. "Everyone makes mistakes. You can get a divorce. I'll wait—"

"David?" Christy's strained voice sounded behind him. "I'm really sorry to interrupt, but your grandfather insisted I come and get you. He's ready to order."

David turned slowly, wondering how much she'd overheard. Even though he'd done nothing wrong, guilt sluiced through him.

"I need to go." David lightly touched Lauren's shoulder. "Will you be okay?"

Lauren stared at him for a long moment. Her gaze darted briefly to Christy before returning to him. "Maybe we can have dinner when you get back to St. Louis?"

She looked so unhappy that David reached up and gave her shoulder a reassuring squeeze. Just because he was married didn't mean they couldn't be friends. "I'd like that."

Lauren leaned forward and brushed her lips across his cheek. "Remember what I said."

Christy stood silently at his side while Lauren got into the cab. They watched her drive off before turning to go inside. David reached for the door handle, but Christy got there first. Jerking the door open, she slipped inside, not bothering to hold it for him. Though he wasn't sure exactly what he'd done, David had the uneasy feeling he'd just messed up again.

David laced his fingers behind his head and watched his wife brush her hair.

Tomorrow morning she'd be on her way back to Chicago and he'd be headed home to St. Louis. Though there was still so much they needed to discuss, they'd barely talked since dinner. Christy had spent most of the evening either on the phone or in front of her laptop.

"Did you get your schedule figured out?" David had the distinct feeling he wasn't the only one with a full calendar.

"I still have a few phone calls to make in the morning." Christy sat on the edge of the bed, the brush flowing through her hair with long sweeping strokes. "I'm trying to free my schedule up for the next month. That way we can spend some time together."

Together. Like last night, he thought.

David sat up straighter and let his gaze linger on Christy. Her blond hair shone like spun gold in the lamplight. And though the shorts and T-shirt she was wearing were more comfortable than sexy, he couldn't stop the feelings of longing that surged through him like a raging river.

He flashed her a suggestive smile.

She didn't seem to notice.

David decided to try the direct approach. "Christy, what do you say we—"

"So, do you think getting together with your old girlfriend is a good idea?" Christy's brush stopped midstroke as if the question had suddenly occurred to her, though he had no doubt it had been on her mind since dinner.

She lifted her gaze, waiting for his response.

David forced a smile and tried to keep a reasonable tone. "I don't see a problem."

"Nothing good can come of it."

"I'm a grown man, Christy." His own mixed feelings about meeting Lauren caused him to speak more harshly than he'd intended. "I'll have dinner with who I want."

To his surprise, Christy merely raised a brow. "I didn't say not to go. I asked if you thought it was a good idea. Lauren is hurting right now."

He couldn't believe it. She'd encouraged him to go to Lauren. Now she was acting as if he was the one pursuing her. "You think talking to me will hurt her more?"

"It could." Christy shrugged and resumed brushing her hair. "But then, you know her better than I do."

Her voice was nonchalant, but her fingers had the brush in a death grip.

David took a deep breath and released it, reminding himself that no one said being married was easy. He moved across the room and sat down next to Christy, taking the brush from her hand. "Let me do that."

He ran the horsehair bristles slowly through her hair, the silken strands soft against his skin. "This is a difficult situation, Christy. I want to do the right thing, for all of us."

"If only we knew what that was," Christy said with a heavy sigh.

"We'll figure it out."

"It's just hard," she said, turning her head to meet his gaze. "Being married to someone you hardly know."

"At least you and I are attracted to each other." His finger traced an imaginary line up her arm. "That's a good start."

She shivered beneath his touch. "Yes, but is it enough?"

"It's enough for now." David dropped the brush to the floor and pulled her onto his lap. She smelled like springtime. He nuzzled her neck, trailing kisses all the way up to her jawline before finding her mouth.

And then something inexplicable happened. As

he felt those soft lips move beneath his own, his heart swelled with an emotion he'd thought he'd never feel again. And David realized with fearful clarity that he'd have to be very careful. Because he couldn't afford to make the same mistake he'd made ten years ago. He couldn't lose his heart again to the one woman who had the power to break it.

Chapter Four

Christy leaned her head back against the seat and stared out the window of the 747. She wondered if she should have tried to call her parents from Las Vegas rather than waiting to tell them in person when they returned to St. Louis from their "around the world" anniversary cruise. But was there really a good way to tell her father that she'd married David Warner?

Though David had always been polite and respectful to her father, her dad had never liked him. When David had broken up with her, her father had tried to act sympathetic, but she could tell he was pleased. And he'd told her that in time she'd realize it was for the best. Over time, she'd convinced herself that he was right.

If they had stayed together, she would never have left St. Louis. The education she'd received at Princeton had been top-notch and the contacts she'd made there had been instrumental in furthering her career. For the past five years she'd been doing a job she loved and, at the same time, furthering God's ministry. How could it get much better than that?

You could have a husband who loved you and a couple of kids who thought you were the best mommy in the whole world, she thought.

Children? Christy had to chuckle. Last week marriage had been a distant dream and now she was thinking of children? Though she hoped a baby or two would be part of God's plan in the future, for now she had to focus all her energies on her husband and making that relationship work before she could even think about bringing a baby into the picture.

Christy made a mental note to call her gynecologist about some birth control pills. Her cycles had always been irregular and the doctor had been encouraging her to go on the pill for years for her endometriosis, but she'd resisted. She wondered if she could start now, even though she hadn't had a period for a while. Though skipping a couple months wasn't unusual for her, she hoped the doctor wouldn't make her come in to see him before he'd prescribe anything.

"Can I get you something to drink?" Though the plane was still boarding, the flight attendant leaned over the seat with a questioning smile.

"A glass of water, please?"

"Certainly."

The flight attendant returned before Christy had a chance to reach into her bag for the tiny pill that she took every morning to regulate her thyroid. She smiled her thanks and took the glass, waving aside the bag of pretzels.

After taking the pill, Christy glanced around the plane. First class was half empty, and she crossed her fingers that no one had been assigned the seat next to her. She had too much to think about on her flight back to Chicago to deal with a stranger.

She'd been married three days. If this were a normal marriage she'd be on her honeymoon, relaxing next to her husband on a beach in the Caribbean. Instead, she was alone on a jumbo jet headed home.

But it wouldn't be her home much longer.

There would be no more jazz concerts in the park or morning runs along the lake. No more saying hello to the guy with the spiked hair at the coffee shop or giving the homeless woman on the street corner an extra dollar or two.

Her heart clenched and she wiped a tear away with the back of her hand.

Is this what I really want to do?

The question had tormented her ever since she'd realized that marrying David hadn't been a dream. She'd tried to be strong and do the right thing. But dear God, she'd be giving up so much.

Not only life in Chicago, a city she'd grown to love, but her dreams of one day marrying a man who loved her with his whole heart. Of carving a future with someone who wanted the same things out of life. Of just being happy.

It didn't seem that much to ask. Perhaps she should have given more thought to David's offer of a quick divorce. At the time she hadn't even considered it. Only now as the shock wore off and reality set in did Christy have to wonder if she'd been too quick to cast that option aside.

Her fans would understand that she'd made a mistake. She'd never pretended to be a saint. She was a sinner and like everyone else she didn't always make the best choices.

It's not too late to call it off.

The tiny voice in the back of her head had grown stronger with each passing hour. Right before she'd gotten on the plane she'd been tempted to tell David she'd changed her mind about staying married.

He'd looked so unhappy when they'd said good-bye. And that made her burden doubly heavy. He'd had his hopes and dreams, too. Would God want them to give up everything just because of one impulsive action? And wasn't it almost sacrilegious to stay together so he could keep control of his company and she could minimize the damage to her career?

Christy heaved a resigned sigh and reached for the phone embedded in the seat in front of her. When she got to Chicago she'd have her attorney draw up the papers. If they rushed it through, David might still be able to marry Lauren before his grandfather's deadline.

But she's not right for him.

The unexpected jealousy took her by surprise. Despite some past problems, Christy knew that Lauren was a good person. And David was a wonderful guy. They'd probably make each other very happy.

Christy stared at the keypad, unable to dial a single number. A single tear slipped down her cheek.

"Can I get you a blanket or a pillow?"

Christy hurriedly dug a tissue out of her pocket and wiped her eyes.

She'd thought the flight attendant had been directing the question to her until a high wavery voice answered, "No, thank you, honey. I'll be just fine."

Christy turned to find an elderly woman with snow-white hair and silver-framed spectacles sitting in the seat beside her. The pale blue eyes behind the lenses sparkled with curiosity. "Hello. I'm Agnes Moore."

"I'm Christy Fair—eh, Warner."

"It's nice to meet you." Agnes smiled and patted the caramel-colored leather. "Isn't this a beautiful plane?"

Christy nodded politely and stifled a groan. Flying over a hundred thousand miles during the past year had made her an expert at spotting a "talker."

"I'm sorry, but I've got this horrific headache." Christy laid her head against the back of the seat and closed her eyes.

It was a risky tactic, and after she'd said it, Christy realized she didn't know why she'd tried it again when it had failed so miserably the last time. On a flight back from Atlanta she'd barely mentioned the word and the middle-aged guy next to her had lit up like a Christmas tree. He'd spent the entire flight detailing his many bouts with "cluster" headaches.

"I'm sorry you don't feel well." The woman patted Christy's hand sympathetically. "My husband used to get headaches, too."

Christy opened her eyes. "Don't tell me. They were the cluster kind?"

"I don't think so." The woman's brows drew together. "I think they were just the plain ones. Tension, I believe is the medical term. I've got some aspirin in my purse. Would you like a couple?"

"Thank you, but I just took some." Christy immediately felt guilty. Why did one lie always seem to lead to another?

"I'm sure you'll feel better soon," Agnes said in a reassuring grandmotherly voice. "Do you want to talk? George often said that talking helped keep his mind off the pain. But I never knew if he was telling the truth or only being kind."

"Kind?" Asking questions would only encourage the woman, but for some reason Christy couldn't stop herself.

Agnes's face turned pink. "George knew how nervous flying made me. Looking back, I suspect he let me chatter as much to help me as to help him."

For the first time Christy noticed the tight grip Agnes had on her black patent-leather purse and the way the elderly woman tensed when the plane gave an unexpected lurch.

"I think keeping my mind off the pain might

help.'' Christy smiled at the woman. ''If you wouldn't mind if we visited...''

Relief flooded the softly lined face. ''That would be lovely.''

Christy thought quickly. Normally she didn't mind talking about herself, but today that was the last thing she wanted to do. ''Tell me about your husband. He sounds like a nice guy.''

''He was.'' A profound sadness filled the older woman's eyes.

''Was?''

''He died the day before Christmas.'' Agnes drew a shaky breath. ''He had a heart attack.''

Christy squeezed Agnes's arm sympathetically. ''I'm so sorry.''

''He went quickly. The doctors said he didn't suffer.'' Agnes unclasped her purse, reached inside and pulled out a lace handkerchief. She dabbed at her eyes before continuing. ''I can't complain. God blessed us with sixty-five wonderful years of marriage.''

Sixty-five years. A lifetime.

Christy couldn't imagine waking up next to a man for all those years and then one day having him not there. ''You must miss him.''

''I can't begin to tell you how much.'' Agnes's eyes took on a faraway look. ''We'd known each other since we were in grammar school.''

"So you were childhood sweethearts?"

"Goodness, no." Agnes's unexpected laugh took Christy by surprise. "Up until I was eighteen I was convinced George Moore was the last man on earth I'd ever want at my side. Oh, he was a good-looking fellow, but much too arrogant for my taste."

"Really?" Intrigued, Christy leaned forward. "How did you two end up together?"

"It was during the Depression. There were eight children in my family and I was the oldest. His father and mine were friends and they farmed next to each other. They decided that George and I should marry. That was it."

"Surely not." Christy's eyes widened. "They wouldn't have just arranged the marriage and not given you a choice."

"Things were different then," Agnes said. "Those were hard times. But they didn't force us. What they were proposing made sense, and we agreed."

"But what was it like?" Christy said softly. "Being married to someone you didn't love?"

"I'd like to say it was wonderful, but that would be a lie. And the only thing I lie about now is my age." Agnes's smile flashed before she turned pensive. "We had a rough year or two."

"How did you make it?"

"Sometimes I wonder." Agnes shook her head, and for a second Christy feared the older woman was going to leave it at that.

But she must have sensed Christy was truly interested, because she took a deep breath and continued. "I don't know about George, but for me it was a couple of things. It started when I made up my mind I was going to be happy. After all, I was going to be married to this man for a long time and what was my alternative? To be miserable and spend my life wishing it was different?"

"You could have gotten a divorce," Christy said. "I know it wasn't as common as it is today, but it was still an option."

"Not for me it wasn't." Agnes shook her head. "When I stood in front of that minister and said 'until death do us part' I made a promise to the Lord. The Good Book says that the Lord will never forsake you and I had to trust that if I stuck to my word, He would stick to His. And He did. In time George and I grew to love each other and we were blessed with many happy years together."

Christy lowered her gaze and pondered the woman's words.

"Are you calling someone?" Agnes gestured to the phone lying in Christy's lap.

Christy's hand rose to the tiny gold cross around

her neck. Could she be as strong as this remarkable woman beside her?

With God's help, anything is possible.

"I was going to, but I've changed my mind." Christy smiled at the woman and placed the phone back in its holder. "I'd much rather talk to you."

Chapter Five

"**M**y dear, this is going to be a banner year." Tom Alvarez, Christy's publicist, raised his coffee cup in a mock salute. "Getting married in Las Vegas on Valentine's Day was a stroke of genius."

Christy took a sip of her iced tea and resisted the urge to tell him again that it hadn't been *planned*, it had just happened. "Have you firmed up any of those talk show appearances?"

Since her marriage last week, Tom had already put together half a dozen deals and was working on several others. He'd been trying unsuccessfully for several years to book her on some of the nationally syndicated talk shows, but until recently they'd showed little interest. Now, since the wedding, they'd been calling *him*.

"Actually..." He lowered his voice as if afraid someone might overhear, even though they were the only customers in the small Chicago café. "I just got the word this morning. It's a definite for Veronica Storm."

"That's fabulous, Tom." Christy couldn't help but be impressed. Veronica Storm was the trendy host of what many considered to be *the* up-and-coming talk show in Chicago.

"I knew you'd be pleased." Tom grinned. "You'll tape the segment in front of a live audience next week."

"So soon?" Christy's mind raced. There were so many details to work out—what to wear, what to say—and a week wasn't that much time. A horrible thought struck her. "I'm supposed to be in St. Louis next week."

"Veronica Storm is your priority now." Tom's tone brooked no argument. "What's in St. Louis, anyway?"

"My husband," Christy said pointedly. "Remember him?"

Actually Christy didn't blame Tom for forgetting. Surprisingly, once she'd returned to Chicago, it had been relatively easy for even her to forget about him. She'd been busy from the time she got up until she sank exhausted into her bed at night.

Only then, just before she fell asleep, did David invade her thoughts.

"How *is* the new hubby?" Tom stirred another packet of sugar into his coffee. "You haven't said much about him lately."

"He's anxious for us to be together." As Christy said the words she wished with all her heart that they were true. In the past ten days she'd spoken to him twice. Once when she'd called to tell him she'd made it back safely, and the other when he'd called to confirm the date her furniture would arrive in St. Louis.

"I can't wait to meet him," Tom said. "He sounds like a great guy."

Christy smiled at her publicist and pushed back a strand of hair with her left hand, the diamond sparkling brightly on her finger. "He is simply wonderful. I'm a lucky woman."

She must have said the words a hundred times since returning to Chicago. They were part of her automatic response whenever anyone asked about her marriage and her new husband.

And every time she said the words, she'd offer up a little prayer that one of these days she'd believe them.

"How long has it been now since you've seen that wife of yours?" Blake took a sip of coffee and peered at David over the top of the cup. "Two? Three weeks?"

David handed the waitress his empty plate and took a deep breath. Blake had been on the attack ever since David had joined his grandfather and cousin for their weekly breakfast planning meeting. Though Blake's barbs had been subtle, they'd hit their mark. But so far David had managed to keep the conversation cordial by reminding himself that Blake had lost his chance to control Warner Enterprises and it was no surprise that he'd be bitter.

"Actually, it's only been a little over a week," David said lightly. "Although it does seem more like two or three. It's hard to be apart."

His grandfather smiled reassuringly. "She'll be back here before you know it."

"I know she will," David said.

"Have you thought what you're going to do if your new bride doesn't like it here?" Blake said. "You can't run the business from Chicago."

"You forget," his grandfather answered before David had a chance to respond. "Christy is married now. Her home is with her husband."

"I agree wholeheartedly." Blake's gaze shifted from the older man to David. "But you know women today. They're not all like Karen. Many of them put all sorts of things before their family."

"Christy's not like that," David said, wishing

he could believe the words. "She's anxious to be back in St. Louis and for us to start building our life together."

"I hope you're right." Blake smiled amicably, but the look in his eyes told David that his cousin wasn't finished with him yet. His cousin may have conceded the battle, but the war was still on.

"You're kidding." Lauren wanted to shout for joy, but she kept her expression carefully neutral. "She's not coming until the tenth?"

"That's right." David leaned back in his office chair, and she could see the strain around his eyes.

Though Lauren longed to slip around the desk and rub his neck, she didn't dare. David had always been an honorable man with a strong sense of right and wrong and she had to tread carefully. But he'd left Christy once, and Lauren had no doubt the relationship between the two of them would falter again. And when that happened she'd be waiting.

"I'm sure she's very busy." Lauren forced a sympathetic tone. "She's got a demanding career, and getting married unexpectedly must have thrown her schedule completely off-kilter."

"You're probably right. I've never known someone so obsessed with planning." The little dimple that Lauren loved so much flashed in David's left cheek and her heart skipped a beat. "You remember how she was. Even in high school that Day-Timer went everywhere with her."

"I'm surprised she doesn't take the thing to bed with her."

"That she doesn't do." David's eyes took on a faraway look and Lauren cursed her impulsive comment.

After all, no good would come of reminding David of the one positive thing about his marriage. Though he'd never breathed a word about his and Christy's sex life, Lauren had seen the way his gaze had lingered on his wife, the longing in his eyes.

If only David had let her show him what he meant to her. Unfortunately a few kisses had been as far as it had ever gone. Lauren knew he liked her, but she had the feeling that she could have thrown herself at him and still he wouldn't have reacted.

But anticipation surged through Lauren at the thought of spending the evening with David. It would be like old times. Maybe it would help him to realize the mistake he'd made.

"It's a pity Christy will miss Sara's party," Lauren said in an offhand tone.

"I think she would have enjoyed meeting everyone," David said.

"You're still going, aren't you?"

David shrugged. "I'm not sure."

"I could pick you up?"

A watchful look filled his gaze. "I don't think that would be a good idea."

"That's fine. I'll just see you there." Lauren leaned back in her chair and smiled.

"If I go," David said.

Lauren merely smiled. He'd be there. David's friendship with Sara was too close for him to ignore the invitation.

With Christy not coming, that night had taken on a whole new meaning, a whole new importance. The way Lauren figured it, this party would be the perfect opportunity for her to make David forget all about his new wife.

"You were spectacular." Tom opened the car door for Christy, smiling broadly. "When did they say it would air?"

"April twentieth is what the producer told me." Exhausted from the taping, Christy slipped inside the car and leaned her head back against the seat. "That was more difficult than I'd thought it would be."

"What was so hard about it?" Tom slid into the driver's seat and put his key in the ignition.

"I don't know. She just had so many questions.'' Veronica had been friendly, but extremely curious. She'd persisted in asking question after question about David. Questions that were difficult to answer when your married life so far had existed only from a few nights in Vegas. Christy shifted in her seat.

''Well, all I can say is you pulled it off.'' Tom smiled happily and Christy knew he was remembering how the woman had put in not one but several plugs for Christy's seminars. ''Want to stop and have a drink to celebrate?''

''It's two o'clock in the afternoon,'' Christy said. She didn't see any reason to tell him that after Las Vegas she'd sworn off alcohol entirely.

''Okay, we'll skip the drink. But we still need to talk.''

Something in her publicist's tone caught Christy's attention. ''What is it, Tom?''

''What's up is we need to decide where we're going from here. We've got to think up some fresh ideas to snag the media's attention.'' Tom put the car in gear and slanted her a sideways glance. ''This marriage of yours is quickly becoming old news.''

''It still seems new to me.'' Christy shook her head. Until she'd met Tom, she'd thought she was the most career-driven person she knew. ''David and I haven't even been seen out together as a couple yet.''

"Being seen out on the town is always good.'' Tom's expression grew thoughtful. "But it's not enough. We need something more. Something newsworthy.''

"Hmm.'' She tried to remember the invitations David had mentioned when she'd called to discuss the furniture delivery. "Let's see. His aunt Dorothy invited us to dinner. The St. Louis Chamber of Commerce is hosting some kind of black-tie event. And, oh yes, his friend Sara Michaels recently got married and is having a party at her home.''

"Sara Michaels?'' Tom sat up straight in his seat. "The Christian singer?''

Christy nodded. "That's the one.''

"You're going.''

"I can't,'' Christy said. "The party is tomorrow night.''

"So?''

"You've obviously forgotten I have an interview with the *Chicago Sun-Times* on Monday.'' Christy couldn't hide her surprise. The interview was for a feature story. It wasn't like Tom to forget something that important. "That's the whole reason I'm staying until next Tuesday.''

"The interview can be done over the phone,'' Tom said.

"It's just a party," Christy said. "What's the big deal?"

"Sara Michaels is red-hot in the music industry right now," Tom said. "At the very least it'll be a good photo op. But I'm going to do my best to see if we can get some air time, too."

"But what if the media isn't interested?"

"Leave that to me." Tom pulled his cell phone from his pocket and handed it to Christy. "Call your husband and tell him your plans have changed. Tell him you wouldn't miss his friend's party for the world."

"Anything else?" Christy asked dryly.

"Yeah, give him a kiss for me." Tom grinned. "This guy is the best thing that ever happened to your career."

Christy stared at the scrap of paper in her hand and glanced at the numbers on the house in front of her.

"Do you want me to wait?" The cabdriver watched Christy in the rearview mirror.

"No, thank you." Christy handed him a couple of bills and opened the door. "I'm meeting my husband. I'll ride home with him."

The man watched Christy straighten her dress and smooth her hair. "Lucky guy."

Though the words were said so softly she wasn't

sure the driver even meant her to hear, they bolstered her sagging confidence and she shot him a brilliant smile. ''I'll be sure and tell him you said so.''

She squared her shoulders and headed up the walk, praying that David was there and that he'd be glad to see her.

Though Tom had urged her to call David, Christy hadn't wanted to promise something she couldn't deliver. She'd waited until she was actually boarding the plane to call him. Unfortunately all she'd gotten was a busy signal.

After she'd landed, Christy had tried again to reach David, but without success. So she'd decided to surprise him. She'd checked in to a hotel and gone shopping for a new dress.

Now she stood in front of a strange house breathing in the cool night air, more scared than excited. Though she and David had attended lots of parties together in high school, this was different. Tonight she felt like a schoolgirl on her first date.

Christy took a deep breath and raised her hand. The door opened before she had a chance to knock.

A ruggedly handsome man with thick dark hair and watchful brown eyes stood in the doorway. ''Sara thought she heard someone drive up.''

His gaze searched her face. Even before he

spoke again Christy could see him trying to place her and coming up short. "I'm Sal Tucci, Sara's husband. I'm sorry, but I don't believe we've met?"

"I'm Christy Fairchild, I mean, Christy Warner. David's wife."

"It's a pleasure to meet you." He smiled and opened the door wide. "Come on in. Last I saw your husband he was over by the fireplace talking to my wife. I'll take you to him."

Christy stepped inside the foyer and glanced around. A cozy blend of contemporary and country, the inside of the home was a marriage of several styles and periods. From the flagstone floor beneath her feet to the hand-stenciled wall treatment reminiscent of Ottoman motifs it all served to give the home an aesthetic lift that Christy found very appealing. "You have a beautiful place."

"Thanks. We haven't even lived here very long, but it already seems like home," Sal said. "Of course, I think I could live anywhere with Sara and it would feel like home."

"That's what it's like when you're in love," Christy said lightly.

"By the way, congratulations on your marriage. I have to tell you it took us by surprise," Sal said. "But we're happy for both of you. And we're happy you could join us tonight."

"I'm glad I was able to make it." Christy smiled and walked with him to an arched doorway.

The long living room was divided into two distinct areas, one a comfortable contemporary arrangement by a fireplace, the second a similar grouping at the opposite end of the space. Between the two areas sat an oak center table.

"Sara." The man at her side called to an angelic-looking blonde standing by the fireplace and motioned for her to come.

The woman smiled a goodbye to her companions and slipped quickly through the crowd to stand beside her husband. He slipped his arm around her and kissed the top of her head.

Christy's heart lurched at the loving gesture.

"I'm Sara Michaels." The blonde extended her hand, not waiting for her husband to perform the introductions.

"Christy Fair—" She stopped herself. "Christy Warner. David's wife."

"Christy!" Sara squealed and gave Christy a quick hug. "I'm so glad you made it. I can't tell you how disappointed I was when David told me you weren't coming. The whole reason I had the party was to welcome you to St. Louis."

Men. Christy returned the hug and swallowed her irritation. David had made this sound like just another party invitation. If she'd known the situation, she would have changed her plans when he'd first asked. And not waited until *Entertainment Today* agreed to send a camera crew.

"Everything fell into place at the last minute," Christy said simply.

"I'm so glad." Sara glanced up at her husband, her face shining. "Can you believe it? David's new wife."

"I know." His smile was indulgent and Christy could tell these two had what she'd always wanted in a marriage. She still hoped that one day her own husband would look at her with eyes brimming with love.

"By the way, where is David?" Sal said.

Christy had just been thinking the same thing. She'd quickly scanned the room when she'd first walked in, but David had been nowhere in sight.

Sara laughed. "I hate to admit this, but he and Lauren are in the kitchen whipping up some of his famous vegetable dip."

A chill that had nothing to do with the temperature of the room traveled up Christy's spine. Lauren had made it clear in Las Vegas that she wasn't giving up on David. Now she was here. *With him.*

It took all of Christy's willpower to force her lips into a semblance of a smile. "How nice."

Sara and her husband exchanged glances.

"They didn't come together or anything," Sara

said quickly. "Lauren was standing there when I asked David if he'd do me a favor and make some of that dip."

"Sara, it's okay. I trust my husband completely." The lie easily slid from Christy's lips. "If you'll just point me in the direction of the kitchen…"

Though Sara appeared reassured, Sal wasn't so easily fooled. He shook his head. "I'll show you."

Christy steeled herself against the sympathy in his eyes. She forced a bright smile. "No, really. You two attend to your guests. I'm more than capable of finding the kitchen."

"If you're sure?" Sara said.

"I'm positive."

"The kitchen is that way." Sara pointed to a hall. "Second door on your right."

"If you run into the camera crew, you've gone too far," Sal said.

"Camera crew?" Christy asked, forgetting for a moment the reason she'd originally agreed to come.

"From *Entertainment Today*." A shadow of annoyance crossed Sal's face. "They've taken over the entire house."

"They have not." Sara chuckled. "Sal's all about security. He doesn't like having strangers in the house. But I've worked with these people before. Actually, they mentioned your name when they called to set up tonight's taping, so I think they'd like to get some shots of us together. That is, if it's okay with you.''

"No problem.'' Christy wished she could be honest and let Sara know how *Entertainment Today* happened to be there in the first place. But if she did, Sara might think the only reason she'd agreed to come had been for the publicity. Of course, that *had* been the original reason, but then, she hadn't known this party was for her.

"Sara—'' Sal squeezed his wife's shoulder "—I'm sorry to interrupt, but Meg is frantically trying to get your attention.''

"My manager,'' Sara said apologetically. She waved at a woman across the room. "She gets kind of stressed.''

"Go on. I'll be fine,'' Christy said. "Don't worry about me.''

"I'm glad you came tonight.'' Sara smiled, her blue eyes clear and direct.

Christy returned the smile, the sincerity in the other woman's tone warming her heart. "I'm glad I did, too.''

She only hoped she could still say that *after* she saw her husband.

David added a slight sprinkling of garlic to the bowl of ingredients. Sara had fallen in love with the odd concoction one year when he'd thrown it together and had brought it to a Super Bowl party. Though he didn't mind making it for Sara, he wished that Lauren hadn't been standing next to him when Sara had asked. Because though Sara's kitchen was spacious, Lauren's hovering was making him claustrophobic.

More than once, he'd been tempted to tell Lauren to go back to the living room and he'd take care of the dip. But she genuinely seemed to be trying to help and he didn't have the heart to kick her out. Still, if she didn't stay out of the way, he was going to have to do something.

He reached for the wooden spoon, but Lauren got there first.

"You want this?" She held up the utensil, dangling it between her fingers, a teasing gleam in her eyes. "Come and get it."

"Lauren, I'm not in the mood for games." David didn't bother to hide his irritation. "If you want to stir the dip, then stir it. Sara's waiting."

"She can wait a little longer," Lauren said. "You haven't told me if you like my dress."

"If I tell you, will you stir the dip?"

Lauren smiled. "I'll think about it."

David heaved an exasperated sigh and shifted his attention to her dress. The garment was an odd shade of red. Though it wasn't a style he particularly liked, he had to admit it looked nice on her. And her perfume had a pleasant scent. He wondered if there was somebody at the party she was trying to impress. "You look nice."

"Is that all?" Her smile couldn't quite hide her disappointment. "Just nice?"

A sense of unease coursed through him. For a second he had the crazy feeling that Lauren was flirting with him. But that couldn't be. She knew he was married. So his first instinct must have been correct. There must be some guy at the party she was interested in and she was feeling insecure and in need of some reassurance.

"Actually, you look fabulous." Because he knew her confidence had been hit hard by his marriage, he laid it on thick. "You're a beautiful woman, Lauren. Any man would be lucky to have you at his side."

"Even you?"

Her lips trembled and his heart twisted. He wished his opinion didn't matter so much to her.

"Even me." David awkwardly patted her shoulder.

Lauren captured his hand with hers and cradled it against her cheek. "I've missed you, David. I can't tell you how much."

"David?"

David's gaze jerked upward at the unexpected feminine voice. He'd thought he and Lauren were alone in the kitchen. But staring into the flashing blue eyes that he hadn't seen in weeks, he realized just how wrong he was.

Chapter Six

Christy swallowed hard and forced a bright smile. "Sara sent me for the dip."

It wasn't quite the truth, but it sounded better than saying she'd come looking for her husband and had found him holding hands with his old girlfriend.

At least Lauren had the grace to blush. "David said you weren't coming."

Christy stared at the woman who'd once been her best friend in high school. "I was able to get an earlier flight back."

"I thought you had an interview Monday with the *Chicago Sun-Times*," David said with a puzzled frown.

"I did," Christy said. Though she hadn't expected David to jump for joy, she'd expected more than this cool reception. "But I decided I'd rather be here with you."

"Really?" Lauren raised a skeptical brow. "I would have thought a chance for publicity would take priority."

"Then I guess you were wrong." Christy met Lauren's challenging gaze with one of her own. "Nothing is more important to me than my marriage."

The door swung open with a clatter before Lauren could respond.

"Are you two going to hang out in the kitchen the whole night?" The intruder's voice rang with mock exasperation. "Everyone's asking about you."

Christy's gaze shot to David. How long had he and Lauren been in here, anyway?

"Rusty, you remember my wife, don't you?" David said, tilting his head in Christy's direction.

The tall redhead shifted his gaze and a flush raced up his neck, turning his face as red as his hair. "I'm sorry, I didn't know——"

"No problem," David said quickly. "You didn't interrupt anything. The three of us were just catching up."

Rusty's gaze returned to Christy. Now that she'd had a chance to study him for a moment, she realized he looked vaguely familiar, though she still couldn't place him.

"I don't believe we've met." Christy extended her hand. "I'm Christy—"

"I know who you are." Rusty made no move to take her hand. "We went to high school together."

"Really?" Christy let her hand fall to her side. "I'm afraid I don't remember you. I don't think I knew anyone in high school named Rusty."

"It's Aaron." David cast the redhead a censuring gaze. "No one except the guys on the baseball team called him Rusty back then."

Aaron.

A light went on in Christy's head. Though she'd never had any classes with Aaron Addison, she knew who he was. He'd been one of David's friends and the guy who'd doggedly pursued Lauren all through high school.

She shifted her gaze and took another look. He'd been a good five inches shorter back then and his hair had been longer and bushier. But it was definitely him.

"It's been a long time, Rusty." Christy offered him a polite smile. "How have you been?"

Rusty ignored her question. His gaze dropped to the ring on her left hand. "I understand you and David got hitched when he was in Las Vegas."

"That's right." The blatant disapproval in his tone took Christy by surprise. She wondered if it was her that was the problem or marriage in general. "So are you married, Rusty?"

"Nope." Rusty cast a sideways glance at David. "I'm not going to settle."

He could have been merely voicing what hundreds of other single men and women said every day. But if that was the case why did his gaze shift to David? And why did David's jaw tense?

"Good for you." Christy lifted her chin. "I don't think anyone should settle on something as important as marriage."

"I agree," David said. He smiled and moved to Christy's side. "I'm glad we waited for each other."

Warmth flowed through Christy at the unexpected show of support. Before she'd left Las Vegas, she and David had agreed to present a united front. And they'd promised to keep to themselves the fact that they weren't ecstatically happy about their marriage. So his words shouldn't have surprised her. But they did.

Christy returned David's smile. His dimples flashed and his arm slipped about her waist.

She breathed in his strong masculine scent and reveled in his closeness. And in that moment, for the first time since she'd arrived in St. Louis, happily ever after didn't seem quite so far out of reach.

Christy stared at the steaming cup of hot chocolate. At the party there had been so many people to talk to, so many people to meet. But since they'd walked through David's front door, it was as if Christy's normally busy tongue had decided to tie itself into knots.

"Having *Entertainment Today* at Sara's party was really a stroke of good fortune." David took a sip of the cocoa and peered at Christy over the top of his cup. "You can't buy that kind of publicity."

A chill traveled up Christy's spine. Did he sound suspicious or was that only her own overactive imagination? Christy took a deep, steadying breath and resisted the urge to chatter mindlessly, something she had a tendency to do when she was nervous.

"No, you can't." Keeping her gaze lowered, Christy took great care stirring the mound of whipped cream into the steaming cocoa.

"Did you know they were there?" David raised a questioning brow. "You didn't seem surprised when Sara came to get you."

"That's because she warned me when I got there." Christy licked the sweet cream off the spoon. "She asked if I'd mind being in a few shots and I said no, that'd be fine with me."

The tension in David's face eased. "You and Sara certainly seemed to hit it off."

The interview segment had gone well because of that fact. The bond that she'd felt with Sara had translated into an easy camaraderie when the camera rolled. Christy nodded. "Sara's great. I can see why she's one of your closest friends. Her husband seems very nice, too."

"Crow's a great guy."

"Crow?" Christy frowned. "I thought his name was Sal?"

David laughed, and once again that dimple she found so cute flashed in his cheek. "Sal used to be an undercover cop, and Crow was his street name."

"Crow." Christy rolled the word around on her tongue and wrinkled her nose. "He doesn't look like a Crow to me."

"You should have seen him when Sara first hooked up with him." David shook his head. "He had hair past his shoulders and a permanent scowl on his face. When she announced they were getting married, everyone was shocked."

"I can't imagine why." The picture David painted didn't jibe with what Christy had seen at the party. "Anyone can see they love each other very much."

"There's no question about that," David said. "In fact, Sara always said it was a match made in heaven. She's made a believer out of me."

"Maybe a year from now they'll be saying that about our marriage," Christy said lightly.

"Our marriage? Made in heaven?" David laughed. "Somehow I have a hard time seeing the Elvis impersonator who married us as God's emissary."

"Remember, the Lord works in mysterious ways," Christy said, fighting to keep a straight face.

"Think about it. Two words," David said. "Elvis. Sin City."

"Actually that's three words." Christy's lips twitched. "But look at it this way, oh ye of little faith—after that kind of start, we have nowhere to go but up."

"Funny you should mention going up." David's hazel eyes shone with a curious intensity. "I was just thinking about going up. Up to bed, that is. Care to join me?"

He stood and circled the table, holding out his hand.

Christy knew what he was asking. A shiver of excitement traveled the length of her spine. She'd realized she'd been kidding herself. She *had* missed him. "Sure, but it'll cost you."

"Cost me?" A frown furrowed his brow.

"Not money, silly," Christy said with a laugh. "I was thinking something more along the lines of a song. I vaguely remember a hunky guy singing 'Love Me Tender' in the Jacuzzi that first night. I'd like a repeat performance."

A hint of red colored his neck. "You can't be serious."

"You did it before," she reminded him.

"Yeah, but I'd also had a little wine."

"C'mon, David," she said with a saucy smile, surprising herself with her boldness. "It'll be a good time."

His gaze fell to the creamy expanse of her neck, then returned to her face. "I've got a much better idea," he said in a soft voice. "Instead of singing, let me show you."

Christy's heart pounded an erratic rhythm. What did he have in mind? Her pulse quickened at the speculation. "'Love Me Tender'?"

"All night long," he said in a low husky tone.

The promise in his tone sent a delightful shiver of longing racing through her. From the beginning this part of her marriage had been perfect.

Christy smiled. Hadn't she often told her seminar attendees how important it was to build on the strengths in a relationship?

She pushed back her chair. "Race you to the stairs."

"Hey, lazy guy."

David stirred but refused to open his eyes even when Christy leaned over the bed and shook his shoulder.

"Wake up. The food will be on the table soon." Her breath tickled his cheek. "If you get up now we can eat breakfast together before we have to leave for church."

"We have plenty of time," David mumbled, and rolled over. "Church isn't until ten."

"Don't give me that. The service starts at nine-thirty," Christy said. "I called."

David groaned and buried his face in the pillow. After being up late last night, he'd planned to sleep in this morning. "Go away."

Christy laughed and with one swift pull jerked off the covers. "Coffee and pancakes will be on the table in two minutes."

David reached down, fully intending to pull the covers back over his head, when the aroma of freshly brewed coffee and hot pancakes hit his nose. After years of breakfast made up of whatever he could eat in the car on the way to work, pancakes fresh off the griddle would be a little bit of heaven on earth. What was an extra hour of sleep compared to that?

Before he could change his mind, David hopped out of bed, grabbed a robe and headed down the stairs. In less than a minute he was seated at the table facing a steaming stack of pancakes dripping with butter and syrup.

"Coffee is coming right up," Christy said with a cheerful smile.

Despite the fact that she couldn't have gotten much sleep, Christy looked amazingly bright eyed. She also looked, David thought with a pang, incredibly beautiful.

Her silky hair that had hung in soft waves to her shoulders last night had been pulled back and secured low on her neck with a pearl clasp. Though some might call her navy dress with jacket conservative, David found the demure cut and style appealing. She'd tied the chef's apron he used for grilling about her waist in a perfect bow.

"What time did you get up?" David lifted a forkful of pancakes to his mouth and immediately discovered they tasted every bit as good as they smelled.

"At seven." She brought two cups of coffee to the table and took a seat.

"Seven?" He lifted his head and stared. "Why?"

"Because I was tired," Christy said matter-of-factly. "I normally get up at five-thirty, but for some reason I just couldn't lift my head off that pillow this morning."

"But this is the weekend." He didn't even bring up the fact that they'd been up most of the night. "Why get up that early?"

"I like to stick to a routine even on the weekends," Christy said. "Over my first cup of coffee I read my daily devotions and watch the sun come up. Then I run on the treadmill and shower. By the time I do my hair and makeup it's time for work."

Though no one had ever accused him of being lazy, it made David tired just to think about it. "But you're self-employed."

"All that means is I have to work harder. If I don't maximize my time and prioritize, there's not enough hours in the day to get everything done."

David laid his fork on the table, the pancakes a leaden weight in the pit of his stomach. His mother had been all about prioritizing, too. David only wished her family could have been higher on her list. Even after all these years he could still hear her standard response: *Not now, David. I have work to do.*

David shoved the memory aside and returned his

attention to Christy. "So, you're telling me you've done all that this morning?"

She nodded. "I even unpacked my suitcases. Thanks again for swinging by the hotel last night. I'd be positively lost without my clothes and makeup."

She sounded so serious David had to laugh. "Don't give me that. You forget that I've seen all of you and you look fantastic."

Their eyes met and the image of Christy with her hair spread loose on his pillow flashed before him. He pushed back his chair, ready to tell her to forget breakfast, that the only place he wanted to be was close to her again.

But before he could speak the clock in the hall chimed the half hour and her gaze dropped to her wrist. Her eyes widened. "Oh, my goodness, we have to leave in thirty minutes. You're not even dressed."

Not being dressed was exactly what he'd had in mind. But the mood in the kitchen had changed, and from the determined look in her eye he knew it would be a waste of time to try to lure her back up the stairs.

David slowly stirred a teaspoonful of sugar into his coffee, trying to hide his disappointment. "I don't recall saying I'd go to church."

"But you have to—"

"Do I?" He lifted the cup to his lips and raised a brow.

"Well, no, I guess you don't," she said. The bright light that had lit her eyes only a moment before dimmed. "I'll go alone."

"Forget what I said. I'll hurry and get ready." David stood and leaned over, brushing an impulsive kiss across her lips.

"Not so fast." Christy rose to her feet and pulled him to her. She kissed him in a slow and leisurely way, weaving her fingers through his hair. When she stepped back, her eyes were dark with emotion and it made him feel better to know he wasn't the only one regretting the lack of time.

David found himself smiling as he pulled on his suit and whistling as they drove across town to the same church he'd attended since he'd been a little boy. It had been weeks since he'd last been there, but when he and Christy walked through the front doors, David felt as if he'd come home.

"David. It's good to see you." Pastor Foster clasped his hand and slapped him on the back before his gaze shifted to Christy. "And who have you brought with you today?"

The sunlight filtering through the stained glass in the foyer danced across Christy's golden hair. Several men standing off to the side cast her admiring glances.

David's arm slipped around her shoulder. "Pastor Foster, this is my wife, Christy."

"Wife?" The young pastor's eyes reflected his surprise. "You never even told me you were thinking of getting married."

"I didn't want to say anything because I wasn't sure she'd have me." David took a deep breath and forced a smile. He hated deceiving the minister, but he didn't see another choice. "We were married in Las Vegas."

"Las Vegas, eh? Well, it looks like you hit the jackpot with this young lady." The pastor reached over and took Christy's hand. "Congratulations and welcome."

"Thank you, Pastor," Christy said.

It took only a moment before Christy and the pastor were chatting like old friends.

David stiffened when she mentioned how much she'd loved teaching Sunday school. He wished he'd thought to warn her not to give the pastor the impression she was interested in being active in the congregation. Getting involved didn't make any sense. It would just be harder on everyone when the year was up and she left.

"...I'd really like to get involved."

It was as if she'd spoken his worst fears out loud. He tried to shake his head, but she was too intent on her conversation to notice.

"Perhaps I could stop by the church office sometime this week and we could talk some more?"

"That would be wonderful." Pastor Foster shot David an approving look. "You're a lucky man."

David smiled at Christy. "That I am."

"Your pastor seems really nice," Christy whispered as they sat down.

"He is," David said. "And he's also a friend of the family. So I'd appreciate it if you didn't mention our little arrangement. I know he wouldn't approve."

Christy lifted her gaze from the church bulletin. "Arrangement?"

He lowered his voice until it was barely audible, careful to make sure that only she could hear. "The needing to stay married for a year thing."

She dropped her gaze back to the folded paper in her lap. "I would never think of telling anyone about that."

"Good." David squeezed her arm. Christy was a good woman. And a beautiful one. She'd make the right man a wonderful wife. It was too bad they were so different. Otherwise he'd be seriously tempted to give this marriage his best shot.

Christy stared down at the list of dates Tom had faxed to her this morning. Though she'd specifically told Tom she wanted to minimize any overnight travel, he obviously hadn't listened.

She tossed aside the paper in disgust, leaned back in the chair and closed her eyes. Though she had a million things to do, lately all she'd wanted to do was sleep. It was definitely avoidance behavior at its best. The stress of the move must finally be getting to her.

Leaving Chicago had been hard. Though she loved St. Louis with all the beautiful trees and friendly people, she had to admit she was lonely.

David had been extra busy since his grandfather had begun the process of turning over the operation of the business to him. His grandfather planned to function as the CEO until next year, when the business would be signed over to David.

Tying David's ownership to a marriage didn't make any sense to Christy. Though she didn't know David's grandfather well, she knew he and his wife had been very much in love. Why wouldn't he want to give his grandson the same opportunity? The old man would have had to know that David couldn't let the company go to Blake, not with his plans to dismantle it and sell it off piece by piece.

Christy brushed back a strand of hair. It was all too confusing and too exhausting to think about.

For now, she needed to finish her e-mail, revise some notes on a presentation and then start supper.

David had made it clear that he didn't expect her to cook and clean, but it was something Christy wanted to do. She wanted to make this house *their* home.

Her parents had both been busy professionals, but they'd done their best to make mealtime special for her and her sister. In their house, the china wasn't reserved for special occasions, and candles and a linen tablecloth were standard fare. The evening meal was a time set aside to share the events of the day and a time to give each other support and encouragement.

Christy was determined to carry over that practice in her own family. But for the past two weeks David had worked late and eaten takeout on the way home. But this morning he'd said he'd be home by six. And she'd told him she'd have dinner waiting.

Tonight they'd begin their own tradition. She hurried through her work, determined to make this meal, and this evening, the best ever.

Chapter Seven

"Good night, Mr. Warner." Joni Thompson, David's administrative assistant, stuck her head inside his office door. "I'll see you tomorrow."

David glanced up. "Don't tell me it's five o'clock already?"

He'd set aside the entire afternoon to review financial reports and he'd hoped to get through them by the end of the day. He still had half the stack sitting in front of him.

Joni smiled. "Actually, it's almost five-fifteen. I have to scoot. Caleb hates it if I'm late picking him up from the sitter."

"Get going, then." David waved her out the door. "Don't keep him waiting."

Joni's life as a single parent was far from easy

and her job often demanded long hours, but David had never heard the woman complain. Since he'd become her boss, he'd vowed to do what he could to minimize her overtime. Consequently, he'd had to assume some of the tasks he would have normally delegated to her. Now he was the one with the late hours. But as soon as he had a firm picture of where the company stood financially, he'd be hiring some extra support staff.

But until then...

David picked up the computer report and shifted his gaze to the tiny rows of numbers.

"Hey, buddy. What's shakin'?" Rusty strolled into the office and plopped into a wing back chair directly in front of David's desk. He still wore his company shirt—a gray polo with "Rusty" stitched in burgundy letters above the pocket. His shift ended at three, but David wasn't surprised to see him still at work. Rusty had been with Warner Enterprises since he got out of high school and he took his job as production crew chief seriously. "What are you still doing here?"

"I could ask you the same question." David shoved the financial reports into a folder and placed them in his top desk drawer.

"Jon Phillips called in sick. I stuck around to make sure the second shift got going okay."

"And?" David lifted a questioning brow.

"Under control." Rusty grunted, giving David a thumbs-up. "Tom Berryman is covering."

"Well, then I think it's time we both call it quits and head for home." David glanced at the clock. He didn't have much time. He'd told Christy he'd be home by six.

"Home? You're not going home." Rusty looked at him as if he'd suddenly grown an extra head. "You and I are going to Adolph's and help Lauren celebrate her birthday."

"Oh, no." David stifled a groan. Lauren had told him more than once to write the date and time of her party on his calendar, but he never had. "Be sure and tell her happy birthday for me."

"Don't tell me you're thinking of not going." The look on Rusty's face would have been comical if the man hadn't been so serious.

"I told Christy I'd be home for dinner." The excuse sounded lame even to David's ears.

"Lauren has been your friend forever." Rusty's unflinching gaze met David's. "You know how much you mean to her."

David wanted to say that was precisely one of the reasons he shouldn't go.

"Look at it this way. If I'm not there—" David paused for emphasis "—maybe she'll finally give you a chance."

"I doubt it," Rusty said. "Since she was sixteen she's only had eyes for you."

David laughed. His friend always had a tendency to exaggerate. "You know that's not true. Lauren has dated lots of guys."

"She may have gone out to an occasional dinner or movie, but you and I both know you're the one she's always wanted." Rusty shook his head. "What I can't understand is why you didn't marry her when you had the chance."

"Rusty," David said, "we've been through this before."

"Yeah, and I still don't get it. Lauren is pretty and smart and fun to be with. She wants to have a big family and to be a stay-at-home mom. Face it, she's what you've said you always wanted."

"But I don't love her."

"So? You married what's-her-name and you don't love her."

"Who says I don't love Christy?" David shot back.

Rusty dipped his head and stared at David. "Give me a break. You hadn't seen her in ten years. And even back then you knew she wasn't the one."

"I was a kid back then. I didn't know what I wanted."

"Yeah, right," Rusty scoffed. "I was there. You knew exactly what you were doing."

David understood Rusty's skepticism. After all, he'd never told Rusty the real reason he'd broken up with Christy. Rusty didn't know that Christy's father had paid David a visit and let him know in no uncertain terms that his relationship with Christy was holding her back. Rusty had no idea that Lauren had confided in him that Christy was thinking of turning down her opportunity to attend an Ivy League school so she could stay near him. And Rusty didn't have a clue that telling Christy he didn't want to see her anymore was the hardest thing David had ever done.

Later he'd realized that their split was for the best. Her father had been right. Christy *was* destined to do great things. And David had come to realize he could never be happy with a career woman for a wife.

Yet I've ended up with one. At least for a year.

"I never understood what you saw in her," Rusty added.

"Christy has always been nice to you," David said. "What do you have against her?"

"She's okay," Rusty said grudgingly. "I mean, I don't hate her or anything. But I guess I never could see how you could prefer her to Lauren."

"Nobody could compare to Lauren in your eyes," David said.

"You're right about that." Rusty paused, and a hint of a smile played at the corners of his lips. "Lauren is…well, she's practically perfect. Unfortunately she's never once looked at me like she looks at you. Even now, I bet all you'd have to do is snap your fingers—"

"Rusty, I'm not snapping my fingers. I'm not giving her any encouragement." David paused. "I'm a married man."

"But for how long? I admit Christy is a knockout and she's probably great in—"

"Rusty." David growled a warning.

His friend continued without skipping a beat. "But that's not going to be enough for you in the long run. You know it's not."

Of course it wasn't going to be enough. Now was the time to tell Rusty the truth. He trusted him implicitly and knew what he said wouldn't be repeated. But something held him back.

Instead David repeated the words he'd said so often they'd become automatic. "I love Christy and we're very happy together."

"Don't give me that." Rusty snorted. "I know you too well."

"Believe what you want." David met his friend's gaze firmly.

"So, are you going to the party or not?"

"I don't think so."

"At least stop by and wish her happy birthday."

David glanced at the clock. Five-forty-five.

"C'mon, David. Adolph's is on your way home." Rusty's voice took on a persuasive edge. "It'll only take five minutes. Can't you spare that for an old friend? 'Cause I'm telling you, if you don't show, her evening will be ruined."

David shoved back his chair and stood. "Why do I have the feeling I'll regret this?"

Rusty's smile widened. "Believe me, the only thing you're going to regret is that we didn't get there in time for happy hour."

David returned Rusty's smile and hoped that this time his friend was right.

The clock chimed seven. Christy blew out the tapered candles that she'd lit in anticipation of David's arrival. She should have snuffed them out long ago. But she'd let them burn even as her hope had flickered. She'd kept her fingers crossed that the next car she'd hear would be his pulling in the drive. But when the minutes had stretched into an hour, what little hope she'd had vanished.

She'd called his office, but no one had answered. His cell phone had automatically gone to voice mail. Where could he be?

He promised he'd be home by six.

But then he'd also promised to love and to cherish her forever. She blinked back the tears that came so easily these days and wrapped up the veal. Though he'd told her more than once that he didn't expect her to cook for him, she'd wanted to make tonight special.

The pineapple upside-down cake had been his favorite when he'd been eighteen. Instead of fine-tuning a presentation she'd be giving next week, she'd spent the afternoon in the kitchen making the cake from scratch and whipping up another of his favorites—twice baked potatoes.

Now just looking at the overcooked spuds turned her stomach. Without a second thought, Christy upended the pan and dumped them all in the garbage.

She returned to the table and gathered up the china and crystal, returning them to the hutch along with her best sterling silver flatware. With precise movements she folded the linen tablecloth and placed it back in the drawer.

By the time she'd changed out of her silk dress and into a pair of running pants and a T-shirt, it was seven-thirty. By the time she'd powered up her computer and reviewed her PowerPoint presentation it was eight o'clock. By the time David strolled through the front door it was almost nine.

"Anybody home?" David's voice rang out from the foyer.

For a second Christy was tempted not to answer, but she knew that would be childish. "I'm in the den."

His footsteps echoed on the hardwood floors. The doorknob turned. Christy lifted her chin.

David stood in the doorway for a long moment, his gaze taking in the paper-strewn desk, the open laptop and the pencil stuck behind her left ear. "Sorry I'm late."

"You were supposed to be home by six." She'd planned to play it cool, but her voice rose despite her best efforts to control it. "I'd have thought in twenty-eight years a smart man like you would have learned how to use a phone."

"I got busy." He loosened his tie and slipped off his suit coat, draping it over the top of the sofa before taking a seat.

"Busy?" His cavalier attitude only incensed her more. "Doing what? You weren't at work. I called."

"No, I wasn't at work." For the first time his cool facade slipped and he shifted uncomfortably in his seat.

"So, where were you?" Christy knew she sounded like a nagging wife, but she was past caring. "I was worried."

"I know you must have been, and I *am* sorry," he said. "Fact is, tonight was Lauren's birthday. Some friends threw her a party and I stopped by. I lost track of the time."

Lauren again.

Christy pressed her lips together and took several deep breaths.

"Next time call," she said finally. She took a moment to straighten the pile of paper in front of her, using the time to regain her composure. "When someone expects you for dinner and goes to the trouble to prepare a meal, calling to say you've been delayed is just common courtesy."

"You made dinner?"

"I told you I'd have dinner waiting for you." No need to mention she'd wasted half the afternoon on that thankless task.

"But you shouldn't have. I mean, I don't expect it." He leaned forward, resting his elbows on his thighs. "I've been taking care of myself for years. I can make my own meals, wash my own clothes, pick up after myself."

"I was just trying to be nice." Christy choked out the words. Up to now she'd done a good job of keeping her composure, but the tears were on their way. Christy snapped her laptop shut, picked up her papers and brushed past him.

"Christy, please, don't go away like this." David reached for her, but she pulled from his grasp and kept walking.

The door slammed shut and David leaned his head back against the sofa cushion. He'd never meant to hurt her or to make her angry. But he had the sinking feeling that he'd done both.

Didn't she understand that there was no point in getting into this married couple routine when it would be over in a year? He'd begun to realize that the closer they got, the harder it would be to say goodbye.

They were already viewed as a couple. A few people at Lauren's birthday party had even asked him when he and Christy were going to start a family. He'd laughed and told them to let him get used to being married first.

Though he wanted to be a father someday, he couldn't help but be grateful that they had both been responsible enough to make sure that wouldn't be happening any time soon. David had watched Christy take a birth control pill each morning they'd been in Las Vegas, so he knew they were safe. And while she was in Chicago, he'd even stopped at a drugstore to pick up some extra protection.

He listened as Christy climbed the stairs and shut their bedroom door. Picking up the remote, David flipped on the television, but turned it off at the first canned laugh. Inexplicably restless, he got up and headed to the kitchen.

Though there had been chips and other snacks at the party, there had been no real food. At this point even cold macaroni and cheese sounded good. David opened the refrigerator door and scanned the shelves. His gaze stopped on a mound of meat covered neatly with plastic wrap, then slid sideways to a large round platter.

Pineapple upside-down cake.

His heart clenched. It had been his favorite for as long as he could remember. In fact, on their last Valentine's Day together, Christy had made it for him. She'd dyed the pineapple red and arranged them to form a big heart. He'd never been able to eat the dessert since without thinking of her. His heart clenched.

David shut the door and leaned against the counter. He'd always prided himself on being a good guy who treated people fairly and with respect. Tonight he'd acted like a heartless jerk. The question was why?

Because you're scared of getting too close.

He railed against the thought even though he knew deep in his heart that it was the truth. And he knew what he had to do about it.

David headed for the stairs.

* * *

Christy stared into the darkness and willed herself to go to sleep. But bitter tears stung the backs of her eyes and her heart felt like a leaden weight in her chest. It seemed every time she tried to take a step forward, a door slammed in her face. She desperately needed someone to talk to, but her parents didn't even know she was married and the last time she'd talked to her sister the three-year-old had chicken pox and the baby was teething. An unappreciated meal paled in comparison.

But Christy knew it wasn't the wasted food that bothered her, it was David's attitude. He acted as if he didn't even like her. And right now she wasn't even sure she liked him.

A tear slipped down her cheek. And then another.

I will be with you. I will not fail you, nor forsake you.

The comforting words from Joshua ran through her mind and Christy hugged them close. She squeezed her eyes shut.

Dear God. I don't know what to do. I want this marriage to work. But just when I think we're connecting, David pulls back. If he could just be my friend, at least that would be a start....

"Christy."

Her eyes popped open at the unexpected voice.

She hurriedly wiped the tears from her cheeks with the back of her hand. "What do you want?"

He crouched by the side of the bed and his face was solemn in the darkness. "I came to say I'm sorry."

Christy shifted her gaze and tried to swallow past the tightness gripping her throat.

"I behaved like a real jerk," he said softly, his breath warm against her face. "You were right. I should have called."

"What's going on, David?" Christy said in a low tone. "Sometimes you act like you like me and other times it's as if you don't care if I'm here or not."

"That's not it at all." David took a deep breath and raked his fingers through his hair. "I like you a lot, Christy, I really do, but chances are you and I aren't going to be together after this year."

A viselike tightness gripped Christy's chest.

"So I'd like it if we could keep it cool. Be friends, but not get too attached." He gave an embarrassed laugh. "It sounds kind of crazy when you say it out loud."

Christy stared, confused. Considering they were married, it did sound kind of crazy. "You want us to live together for the sake of appearances, and just bide our time until the year is up?"

"I was hoping we could be friends, too," he said.

Christy was tempted to say no, to say she couldn't live like that, but she hesitated. She remembered her prayer. "I guess we could give it a try."

"Good." Satisfaction filled David's voice. "You won't be sorry."

"There's something I need to make clear," Christy said, propping herself up on one elbow. "You may want us to be just friends, but we are married, so no other women."

Surprise flickered across his face. "That goes without saying."

"I just wanted to be sure that we were on the same page," Christy said.

"Understood. No other men for you. No other women for me," he said. David held out his hand. "Friends?"

She took his hand and shook it firmly. If he just wanted to be friends, friends it would be.

At least for now.

Chapter Eight

When Christy woke up, David was gone. A note on the bedside stand said he'd moved his clothes down the hall to the guest bedroom. Obviously he hadn't wanted to presume on their "friendship." Christy crumpled the paper into a little ball with one hand and tossed it into the trash, shrugging aside her disappointment.

Today she would take Agnes's advice and be happy. She had a lot to be thankful for and there was no need to focus on the negative. She had a whole list of things to do, and right now keeping busy would be her salvation.

Hours later, Christy sat at the desk in the den staring at the computer screen. She'd spent the morning paring a four-hour presentation down to two, but now she worried that she'd cut too much of the "meat" and left too much "fluff."

Putting on a quality seminar was something Christy took seriously. Though the people in the audience might have registered for different reasons, they'd given up their time and money to attend and she wanted to make sure it was a worthwhile experience.

She rearranged the opening for the third time and read through it again. Frowning, she leaned forward and stared at the first few sentences. Something still wasn't right. She liked to grab the audience right from the beginning, and her opening gambit had all the pizzazz of a chemistry textbook.

A twinge in her back reminded her why her mother had always insisted she sit up straight. Christy shoved back the chair, rose and stretched, her eyes straying to the bright sunny day outside her window.

She glanced down at the running pants and T-shirt she had pulled on after her morning shower. When she'd lived in Chicago she'd run outside every day it didn't snow. Since moving to St. Louis, she could count on one hand the number of times she'd been out. And she suddenly realized how much she'd missed it.

She was tempted to pull on her running shoes

and just head out the door, but there was no way she could leave the room in such a mess.

With a resigned sigh, Christy turned back to the cluttered desk. In a matter of minutes she'd stowed the computer out of sight in the bottom desk drawer and turned her attention to the mounds of papers on the desktop. She'd barely finished putting them neatly in the leather briefcase her parents had given her for college graduation when she heard the front door open.

Her head jerked up. The cleaning woman wasn't scheduled until the afternoon. Christy moved silently to the door, her heart pounding in her chest.

"Anybody home?" David's voice rang out from the foyer.

"I'm in the den," she answered, relief coursing through her veins.

But instead of going to greet him as she would have yesterday, Christy grabbed a magazine from the end table and took a seat on the couch.

It wasn't long before David stood in the doorway, looking way too handsome for eleven o'clock in the morning.

"What are you doing home?" she said, forcing her gaze back to the bright deodorant advertisement.

"That's what I call a warm welcome."

"I'm just surprised to see you," she said casually. "You've never stopped home during the day before."

"It's too nice a day to spend inside." He paused, and she looked up to find his gaze fixed on her. "Want to go to lunch? My treat."

"I'm afraid I'll have to pass. I was just getting ready to go for a run." She gestured to the briefcase next to the desk. "I'm having trouble concentrating, and I'm hoping it will clear my head."

David's face fell. "I should have called."

"You could come with me?" she said impulsively.

"Me?" He lifted a brow. "Run with you?"

She smiled. The idea was growing on her. "If you remember, we used to run together."

"Don't remind me," he said with a chuckle. "You were always faster than I was."

She smiled, knowing it was true. "C'mon, it'll be fun."

Fun, David decided, was relative. He enjoyed being outdoors, but matching Christy stride for stride really took it out of him. Obviously, playing golf twice a week didn't translate into physical fitness.

Up ahead, he caught a glimpse of a trailside café he'd eaten at once or twice. Though the food had never been particularly good, after three miles of running he thought it looked mighty appealing.

"Let's stop and grab some lunch." He cast a sideways glance at Christy and slowed his pace. "I skipped breakfast and I'm starved."

"I had a big breakfast, so I'm really not hungry." Her pace edged down a notch to match his. "But an iced tea does sound good."

But once they were seated at a table next to a tall oak tree, Christy changed her mind and ordered a club sandwich.

"I probably should have told the waitress to hold the mayo," she confided as the woman left to put in their order. "I certainly don't need the extra calories."

"You don't have an ounce of fat on your body," David said, his gaze lingering on her slender form. "I can testify to that."

Her cheeks turned pink. "Well, I will if I don't stop eating so much. For some reason, since I moved to St. Louis I'm always hungry."

"It's all this fresh air." David smiled. He'd noticed she had quite an appetite, but he liked a woman who enjoyed her food.

"St. Louis is so beautiful." Christy's gaze scanned the wooded area next to the trail. "I'd forgotten how many trees there are here."

"Do you miss Chicago?" He suddenly realized

they'd never talked about the sacrifice she'd made in moving back to Missouri.

"Parts of it," she admitted. She pushed back a strand of hair that had pulled loose from her ponytail. "I really miss my friends. The girls I knew here in high school have long since moved away and there really isn't anyone left."

David thought about pointing out that Lauren was still in town, but decided against it. "What about Sara? You two seemed to hit it off. Why don't you call her up? Set up a time to go shopping or something?"

Christy shrugged. "I don't know her well enough to feel comfortable doing that. She's busy recording a new album and she has tons of friends. Not to mention a new husband."

"How about—"

"David." She covered his hand with hers. "Don't worry about it. I'm a big girl. I'll be fine."

The waitress brought their food and Christy smiled her thanks and changed the subject. He listened with half an ear as she chattered on, thinking how pretty she was and how she always looked on the bright side. She'd been like that even at eighteen. It had been one of the things he'd loved about her. That, and her passion for life.

He wondered what would have happened if they had stayed together. Would they have ended up married? Or would they have eventually split up and gone their separate ways?

It was odd that they'd bumped into each other after all these years. They certainly hadn't parted on the best of terms. He hoped this time they could part more amicably and remain friends. Because he was just beginning to realize how nice it was to have Christy back in his life.

David glanced around the coffee shop that Sara had picked for their impromptu meeting. The walls were covered with antique signs and little shelves with scraps of lace. He shifted in the Windsor armchair and smiled across the table.

"I'm glad you could meet me." David added another teaspoonful of sugar to his coffee. "It's too bad Sal couldn't come."

"From what I understand his company is having some problems with a security system they're installing and my dear husband has decided he needs to be personally involved," Sara said with a fond smile.

"Does he ever miss the police force?" David asked. Sara's husband had been an undercover police officer for years and it wasn't until after he'd met Sara that he'd left the force and started his own security company.

"I don't think so," Sara said. "He was ready

for a change. How about Christy? Does she miss Chicago?''

''That's what I wanted to talk to you about.'' David took a sip of coffee, then set down his cup, choosing his words carefully. ''I've had to work a lot of hours since I took over the business and that means she and I haven't been able to spend as much time together. This is the slow season for her job and if you want the truth, I think she's a little lonely.''

Sara's face softened in concern. ''First let me remind you that she is your priority, not your job.''

David shifted uncomfortably. What Sara said would have been true *if* he and Christy had a real marriage. ''I know that.''

''That being said, tell me what I can do to help?'' Her blue eyes met his and he had to smile at the intense scrutiny in her gaze.

''Call her up and ask her to go shopping,'' he said promptly. ''Take her to the Galleria and blow a couple hundred dollars.''

''A couple of hundred?'' Sara gave him a pitying glance. ''You really don't go shopping that much, do you?''

''So you'll do it?''

''What are friends for?'' Sara said with a smile. ''Besides, I like Christy and it will be a good chance for us to become better acquainted.''

"How can I thank you?"

Sara's expression turned serious. "You can take good care of her, David."

He smiled. Of course he'd take good care of Christy. He wanted her to be happy. After all, it would be a year before she'd move back to Chicago. When she returned to the Windy City David wanted her to be able to look back on this time in St. Louis with fondness, and not regret.

Blake's heart picked up speed. Normally his wife's gossip bored him silly, but not today. When she'd first mentioned that their cleaning lady had talked to the woman who cleaned David's house, he'd thought he was going to be hit up for more money. Instead he'd hit pay dirt. "What else did Celeste say?"

"Just that Suzanne—that's David's cleaning lady—said that David and Christy sleep in separate rooms." Karen's brow furrowed. "Doesn't that seem strange for newlyweds?"

Not if their marriage is a sham solely for the purpose of stealing the company from me, Blake thought.

"It does seem odd," he said, careful not to show too much interest. His wife liked Christy, and she just might clam up if she thought what she said would be used against her. "But I'm sure there's some logical explanation."

"That's what I thought, too," his wife said with a sigh of relief. "Maybe David snores. Who knows?"

Blake smiled. The information had only confirmed his suspicions. Now that he knew, all that was left was to decide what to do about it. And when to make his move.

Chapter Nine

Lauren opened her closet door and took out the pale mint-colored gown. She'd had such high hopes when she'd ordered the dress. In her mind, she'd envisioned making a grand entrance at the gala with David on her arm and a huge diamond ring on her finger.

She blinked back the sudden tears. How had it happened? Just when had her dream appeared so close she could almost taste the wedding cake, it had been snatched away.

Ever since she was sixteen she'd been in love with David Warner. It had broken her heart when he'd started dating her best friend. Of course, she couldn't blame David or Christy. Back then, she hadn't told either of them how she'd felt. So while her heart was breaking, she'd pretended to be happy for both of them. But all she could think of was that she could make David happier than Christy ever could.

When Christy's desire to attend Princeton had warred with her desire to stay in state and be close to David, Lauren hadn't tried to influence her. Though she had prayed every night that Christy would pack her bags and move to New Jersey.

But when David had noticed Christy's preoccupation and come to Lauren, she'd had to tell him the truth, hadn't she? He'd had the right to know that he was the one thing standing in the way of Christy accepting the scholarship.

And who could say why David really had broken up with Christy? It could have been for any number of reasons. All Lauren knew was that David was then a free man, and when she brought up the senior prom and he'd asked her to go with him, what could she say but yes?

Christy had refused to understand that her agreeing to go with David had nothing to do with their friendship. Lauren understood that Christy still had feelings for David. But he'd broken it off and if Lauren didn't go with him to the dance, there were a dozen other girls who would.

The only problem was that no matter how hard she tried, she couldn't seem to make David fall in love with her. But she'd decided it didn't matter. He cared for her, he liked her and she had enough love in her heart for both of them. And once they were married she firmly believed that he would grow to love her, too.

But then he'd seen Christy and in an instant it was all gone. He'd taken leave of his senses and...

A tear slipped down her cheek. Lauren wiped it away and reminded herself that no one got through life without making a few mistakes. David had made a big one when he'd impulsively married Christy, but that didn't mean he had to pay for the rest of his life.

Lauren lifted her chin. All she'd ever wanted to be was David's wife and the mother of his children. She'd invested ten years of her life in him and she certainly wasn't going to give up now.

One way or the other she would get him back. She was going to wear this dress to the gala and show David just what he was missing.

David eased into his office chair and turned on his computer, exhaling a sigh of relief. It felt so good to just sit.

For the third day in a row he'd risen at six to accompany Christy on her morning run. They didn't talk much, but the easy camaraderie that had existed years ago between the two of them had returned. He smiled in satisfaction. Their friendship was off to a good start.

He picked up the phone just as Rusty swaggered through the doorway, a broad grin on his face.

"Aren't you going to ask me why I'm smiling?" Rusty sank into a nearby chair and exhaled a long sigh of contentment.

David set his pencil down on the desk and leaned back. He hadn't seen his friend this happy since they'd won the office two-on-two basketball tournament a couple of years ago. "No."

"Why not?"

"Because I have the feeling you're going to tell me anyway."

"But I want you to ask me," Rusty insisted.

"O-kay." David sat back in his chair and forced a serious expression. "Rusty, why are you smiling? Did you find out you're getting money back from your income tax? Or could you have won the lottery?"

Rusty's grin widened. "Better than that."

David sat forward and lifted a questioning eyebrow.

"Lauren said she'd go with me to the Spring Gala."

"No kidding? That is good news." David didn't know what had contributed to Lauren's change of heart, but he couldn't help but be happy for Rusty...and for himself.

The Spring Gala was Warner Enterprises' big yearly event and for the past few years Lauren had gone as David's date. In fact, Lauren had told him just before they'd left for Las Vegas that she'd already bought her dress for this year's event.

"I really didn't think she'd go, but I thought about what you'd said the other day—about maybe now with you out of the picture she might be willing to give me a shot—and I thought what did I have to lose?" Rusty leaned forward and rested his elbows on his knees. "Still, you could have blown me away when she said yes."

"Maybe things will work out for the two of you," David said, hoping that would be the case. Even after all the years he'd spent with her, the thought of Lauren with another man didn't bother him in the least.

"I don't know 'bout that," Rusty said. "But at least she's giving me a chance."

"You've definitely got your foot in the door."

"Thanks to you and that Las Vegas wedding." Rusty rose. "I'd better get back to work." He strode to the door and stopped. "You know, I'm liking that new wife of yours more and more every day."

David smiled and watched his friend head down

the hall. He was glad for Rusty. Glad that Lauren was giving the guy a second look.

Because Lauren was a good person. And so was Rusty. They both deserved to be with someone who loved them.

Heck, didn't everyone deserve at least that?

"You'll never guess who called me today." Christy sat back in the kitchen chair and watched David put his TV dinner into the microwave.

David punched in the time and pushed the start button, wishing he hadn't made such a point about making his own dinner. "Who?"

"Sara." Christy's lips curved in a smile. "We're going shopping tomorrow."

He could hear the happiness in her voice, and it only reiterated that he'd done the right thing in talking to Sara. Pulling a carton of milk from the refrigerator, he poured himself a glass and then took a seat opposite Christy. "Are you two going to be looking for anything special?"

"Maybe something for that Spring Fling, or whatever it is you call that office party," she said thoughtfully. "Though I'm not sure exactly what kind of dress I should be looking for."

"Actually it's called the Spring Gala," he said. "And it's formal, though you'll see a little bit of everything."

"Formal?" Christy's eyebrows rose. "That surprises me."

"Why?" David got up and took his dinner out of the microwave.

Christy paused. "Don't take this wrong. But most of the people that work at Warner are blue-collar. I can't imagine that they'd be interested in wearing a tux or a formal gown."

"That's where you're wrong," David said. "We promote it as a prom for adults and it's our most popular event. For many this is their only chance to dress up and dance to live music."

"It sounds like fun," Christy said.

"You don't have to come if you don't want to."

"Not want to?" Christy frowned. "Why wouldn't I want to?"

David paused, but knew she needed to know. "Lauren will be there."

"She doesn't work for Warner."

"No, but Rusty does and she's coming as his date."

"And why should that bother me?"

"I know seeing her at Sara's party made you uncomfortable."

"Seeing you holding hands with her is what made me uncomfortable." Christy raised a brow. "I assume she won't have her arms around you at this party."

"Only if she cons me into dancing with her."

"Well, then I guess I'll just have to make sure I keep your dance card full." Christy leaned over the table and smiled impishly. "After all, what are friends for?"

David grinned and tore the plastic topping off his dinner. He had the feeling this gala was going to be very interesting indeed.

"Thank you so much for helping me find the dress." Christy glanced at the garment bag folded neatly over the chair next to her.

"No problem." Sara smiled as the waiter set two Italian sodas on the table. "I love shopping."

"Me, too." Christy took a sip of the soda. "And I love having someone with me to tell me what looks good and what looks hideous."

Sara laughed. "I don't think there was one thing that you tried on that looked hideous."

"You're forgetting perhaps the aqua-colored taffeta," Christy said, remembering how she'd looked in the three-sided mirror. "The one the clerk insisted I try on?"

"She probably could have gotten an extra bonus if she'd sold it." Sara's laughter mingled with Christy's. "You're right. That dress *was* ugly."

They were still laughing when a woman Christy had never seen before approached the table.

Dressed in a cream-colored linen sheath with matching jacket, the thirtysomething-year-old looked more ready for work than shopping.

Christy suddenly felt underdressed in the khaki pants and cotton sweater that had seemed perfect only moments before.

"Sara, what are you doing in town? I thought you and Sal were in Bermuda."

"Nancy, what a surprise." Sara's smile was warm and welcoming. "Actually, we put our vacation on hold. This new album is taking more time than I planned. How have you been? And how's Rick?"

"I'm doing great. And Rick, well, he's been working a lot."

Sara gestured to an empty chair. "Won't you join us?"

"Well, I do have a few minutes before I need to pick up Amy from school." Nancy hesitated, her gaze shifting to Christy. "If you're sure I won't be interrupting."

"You're not interrupting anything at all," Christy said. "Please join us."

"In that case, I'd love to." The woman took a seat and smiled at Christy. "I'm sorry, I don't believe we've ever met. I'm Nancy Hunter."

"I am so sorry," Sara said, clearly embarrassed. "I thought you'd met Christy at my party."

"Unfortunately I couldn't attend," Nancy said. "Until a few days ago I've been in Minnesota helping my mother get settled into a new apartment."

"That's right. Sal did tell me that." Sara smiled at Christy. "Christy Warner, Nancy Hunter. Nancy's husband, Rick, works with David. He's a CPA."

"It's a pleasure to meet you," Christy said, shaking Nancy's hand.

"Warner?" Nancy's brows drew together in a frown. "Your last name is Warner?"

Christy nodded.

"So you must be…?"

"David's wife," Christy said.

"But how can that be?" The shock on the woman's face would have been laughable at any other time. "I thought he and Lauren—"

Nancy stopped suddenly as if she realized what she'd been about to say.

Sara shot Nancy a warning glance.

Christy wasn't sure how she managed it, but she kept a smile on her face.

"Christy and David have known each other since high school," Sara said.

Nancy turned to Christy, her expression clearly contrite. "I'm so sorry. The news just took me by surprise. I'm really happy for you both."

Christy couldn't hold it against her. If she'd been in Nancy's position she would have been shocked, too. "So your husband works with David?"

"Yes, Rick's been there almost ten years," Nancy said. "And he and David are golfing buddies. They have been for years. But I'm sure you already know that."

Actually Christy had no idea who David golfed with or even that he played at all. "Hopefully I'll be able to convince David to play a few rounds with me. I haven't played in years, but I'd like to get started again."

Sara stared at Christy in surprise. "You never told me you golfed."

"It never came up," Christy said.

"Sara and I golf together in a women's league." Nancy's gaze shifted briefly to Sara. "We're looking for another woman to round out our foursome. One of our team members just moved to Arizona. Would you be interested?"

"It sounds like fun," Christy said. "But it would be hard for me to commit to being there every week. I travel for my job and my schedule can be pretty erratic."

"That's okay," Nancy said. "When Sara's touring she's gone more than she's there. But that's what subs are for."

"Okay, count me in." At the very least, it would be a good way to meet some other women and a good opportunity to get to know Sara and Nancy better.

"By the way, who's the other one on the team?" Christy turned to Sara. "Is she someone I've already met?"

"It's Lauren," Sara said.

Nancy stared from Christy to Sara. "Is that a problem?"

"A problem?" Christy took a sip of her soda and forced a smile. "Not at all."

It wasn't until Nancy had left to pick up her daughter at school and Christy and Sara were on their way back to Sara's house that Christy brought up the subject again.

"I'm not sure if golfing on the same team as Lauren is such a good idea."

Sara slanted a sideways glance at Christy. "It might be a little awkward at first. But I'm sure it would get better over time."

"I'm not so sure."

"I thought you two used to be good friends?" Sara said. "What happened, anyway?"

"David happened," Christy said.

"But that's all in the past," Sara said. "Lauren understands that."

"I'm not so sure she does."

"Surely you don't think she'd want him, knowing he's married."

"I think she'd take David any way she could get him."

"Well, it doesn't matter how much she wants him," Sara said. "Because it's not going to happen."

"And why is that?"

"Because David loves you," Sara said promptly. "After all, he married you, not her. You don't have a thing to worry about."

Christy smiled, only wishing she could have such faith in David's love…and in her marriage.

Chapter Ten

Christy pulled the door shut behind her and heaved a heavy sigh. The workshop she'd put on for a consortium of local churches had gone well, but by the time five o'clock had rolled around she'd been ready to drop.

She set her briefcase on the side table and hung her jacket in the closet. The aroma of frying bacon filled the air. Though she hadn't eaten since breakfast, the greasy smell made her stomach turn.

"Christy." Wearing a pair of faded jeans and a St. Louis Cardinals sweatshirt, David stood in the doorway leading to the kitchen, looking incredibly handsome. He flashed her a welcoming smile. "You're just in time. I made bacon and eggs for dinner."

Just the thought of eggs swimming in grease was enough to turn her stomach. She swallowed hard against the bile rising in her throat.

"No, thanks." She waved a dismissive hand. "I'm really not that hungry."

"Why don't you join me anyway?" he said. "It's no fun eating alone."

Bone tired, Christy glanced longingly up the stairs. She'd planned on taking a quick nap before dinner. She shifted her gaze back to David, prepared to tell him to eat without her, but the hopeful look on his face made her hesitate.

"At least have some toast and coffee," he said in a persuasive tone that she found hard to resist.

Christy thought for a moment. Maybe she *would* feel better if she got something in her stomach. "Sure. Why not?"

She followed him back to the kitchen, surprised to find a linen cloth blanketing the table and silver at each place setting. "What's all this?"

David's smile turned sheepish. "I knew your seminar ended at five. I didn't know if you were coming straight home or not, but I thought if you did it'd be nice if we ate together."

She tried to conceal her surprise. "I'd like that."

David moved to the stove and scooped two eggs and several strips of bacon onto a plate. Golden-brown bread from the toaster followed. He offered the overflowing plate to her.

Christy smiled weakly and shook her head. "I'm just going to have toast and coffee. I'm not into fried eggs. I like mine poached or hard-boiled."

"I'm afraid I didn't make any poached, but I do have a few hard-boiled ones."

Christy raised a questioning brow.

"The eggs were getting old and I thought I'd have egg salad for lunch tomorrow."

"You can make egg salad?" Christy couldn't keep the surprise from her voice. The most cooking her father had ever done had been starting the automatic coffeemaker.

"Actually I'm quite a good cook," David said. "Not only can I boil eggs, but I make a great lasagna and a mean vegetable dip."

"You're amazing, David Warner," Christy said in a light tone. "A true Renaissance man."

"Let's just say I'm a guy who likes to eat," David said, setting a dish with two hard-boiled eggs and a plate of toast in front of her.

Christy smiled her thanks and tapped her spoon against the eggshell. "Tell me about your day."

David pulled up a chair and took a seat across from her at the table.

"We always talk about me," he said. "I want

to talk about you. Tell me about this seminar you did today.''

Christy wondered what had brought about this transformation. But she decided not to question the turn of events. ''We had a full house—almost two hundred and fifty. The program focused on the importance of communication.''

''That sounds interesting.'' David munched on a strip of bacon and leaned forward. ''But communication is such a broad topic.''

''You're right.'' Christy took another bite of toast, grateful that her stomach was finally settling down. ''What I did was emphasize strengthening certain communication skills in marriage.''

His eyes met hers. ''Such as?''

''What you're doing now,'' Christy said.

David raised a brow.

''I'm serious,'' she said with a smile. ''At this moment you're giving me your full attention. That says to me that you're interested in what I have to say and that I'm important to you.''

''I *am* interested in what you have to say,'' David said. ''And you *are* important to me.''

A warmth flowed through her at his words, and Christy once again realized firsthand the power of words.

''You're important to me, too,'' she said softly.

''Christy.'' He pushed the eggs around on his

plate with the side of his fork. "I'm sorry about all this mess."

She glanced around the kitchen. Granted, the toaster still sat on the counter and the skillet hadn't been cleared from the top of the stove, but the room was a far cry from being a mess. "It doesn't look that bad—"

"Not the kitchen," he said, lifting his gaze. "I'm talking about this whole marriage business. I hope you know I never meant to hurt you."

Christy started to say that it was okay, that she knew he never meant to hurt her, but she stopped herself. All she could think of was how she'd warned her seminar attendees that nothing shut down true communication more than giving trite, pat answers.

For days she'd prayed for an opportunity to re-open a true dialogue with David. Now that she'd been given the perfect chance, why was she finding it so hard to find her voice?

"After the way I treated you all those years ago, I don't understand how you could have even considered marrying me," David added.

Christy's gaze dropped to her plate. Even after ten years, remembering how he'd dumped her without a second thought still hurt. He'd been her whole world. In one day she'd gone from thinking she knew him better than she knew herself to being convinced she hadn't known him at all.

"I married you because in some way I'd never stopped loving you," she said finally. "And for that brief moment in that lounge in Las Vegas, I was willing to let my heart lead the way." She gave a little laugh. "I know it doesn't sound like me. I've never been much of a gambler."

Christy had taken a chance and spoken from the heart. She only hoped her honesty would encourage David to do the same.

He paused and cleared his throat.

"You've always been a risk taker," David said, meeting her gaze. "It took great courage to leave your family and go off to New Jersey alone when you were only eighteen."

"What was hard was leaving you," she said softly.

He stared at her for a moment. "Not as hard as it was to let you go. When I watched your plane take off, I didn't think I'd ever see you again."

Christy frowned. Her parents had been at the airport, but she and David had split up months before. Unless…

"You were there?" she asked, even though she already knew the answer. "You came to see me off."

David gave a reluctant nod.

"But why?"

"It doesn't matter." His eyes took on a faraway look.

"It matters to me," she said.

He remained silent.

Her heart flip-flopped in her chest. Why would he have come to see her off unless he'd still cared?

"Why did you break up with me, David?" Thankfully her voice came out matter-of-fact instead of weak and trembly like her insides. "We were so good together."

He reached forward and took her hand. "You're a wonderful woman and I know that one day you'll find the right man and have a long and happy life together."

"But I'm married to *you*."

David's hazel eyes darkened and a look of regret filled his gaze. "No matter how much we'd like it to be different, we can't kid ourselves," David said. "You've got this great career that keeps you incredibly busy and I don't know whether I'm coming or going at mine. If we had children, who'd take care of them? We both have enough trouble looking after ourselves."

"Your mother had a career." Christy fully supported a woman's right to stay home, but she'd never envisioned herself in that role. "So did your father."

"My mother," David said, speaking slowly and distinctly, "may she rest in peace, was a wonderful woman. But she was on the road more than she was with her family."

Christy thought of her own schedule. Though she tried to keep her travel to a minimum, she still spent close to twenty percent of the time out of town. "I'm not sure what the fact that we're both busy professionals has to do with anything. Lots of couples lead busy lives."

"I know that," he said. "I grew up in that kind of household and I don't know if it's fair for kids to always come in second to their parents' careers."

"But that's positively archaic," she said.

"Or is it just being honest?" He raised a brow. "Don't you talk in your seminars about the importance of putting God and family first?"

"I do put God first." Christy lifted her chin, ignoring the twinge of doubt about the family part of David's question. "I serve Him every time I take center stage. And I'm home a lot of times when you're gone. You can't honestly tell me that you feel I've neglected you."

"No, of course not," David said. "But don't tell me you haven't thought about how nice it would be to have someone there waiting at home for you after a long day?"

Christy couldn't help but smile thinking what it would be like to have David there waiting.

"And think about when you have children," he continued. "Children need their mother to be available. And I've never believed all those arguments about quality versus quantity stuff."

"What I believe," Christy said, "is that *both* parents have to make sacrifices for their children."

"For the next few years my job is going to take most of my time and energy," David said. "Even if I want to, I won't be able to make sacrifices. That's why I couldn't believe my grandfather tying my taking over the business to having a wife."

"We all need balance in our lives," Christy said, resorting to the same persuasive tone he'd used so effectively earlier. "There's no reason we can't come up with a workable solution."

For a second indecision crossed his face. Then he shook his head.

"I don't know how I can do more than I'm doing, unless I give it all up." David heaved a resigned sigh. "And if I'm not willing to make sacrifices I can't ask you to, either."

"Maybe I could cut back a little after we had children?"

David shook his head. "I know that you think—"

"What if I wanted to?" she interrupted.

"My mother promised my dad all sorts of things before I was born," David said. "But after six weeks of being home with me she told him she was going stir-crazy. She went back to work part-time initially just to 'get out of the house,' but within six months she was back working full-time and traveling more than ever."

"I would never do that," Christy protested.

"You do so much good in your work," he said. "It would be hard for anyone to walk away from all that."

"We could wait to have children."

"For how long?" David said. "We're both almost thirty. And what's going to change? If anything, our lives will only get busier."

Christy stared at his handsome features and disappointment squeezed her heart. Was she only fooling herself when she dreamed of having it all?

"So you're saying that the only way you can see yourself happily married is if it's to a woman who doesn't work outside the home?"

David slowly nodded.

"I guess that's it, then," she said with a heavy sigh.

David reached over and took her hand. Her breath caught in her throat at the depth of pain reflected in his gaze.

"You deserve so much better," he said. "I can't tell you how sorry I am about all of this."

"Why *did* you marry me, David?" she said.

He glanced at his plate before he lifted his gaze and met hers. "I married you because I've always loved you."

She widened her gaze. "You love me?"

"Since the first moment I saw you," he said. A hint of red touched his cheeks as if he was embarrassed by the admission. "That's why I could never bring myself to marry Lauren. I kept waiting to fall in love, but now I understand why that never happened."

Christy raised a questioning brow.

"Because I'd already given my heart to you."

Joy bubbled up inside Christy. "That's wonderful."

"Wonderful? What's so wonderful about it?" David raked his fingers through his hair. "It just makes everything more complicated."

"No, it doesn't. Don't you see?" Christy leaned across the table and took his hand. "It makes it simpler."

David shook his head slowly. "Loving each other doesn't change anything."

He was wrong. The fact that he loved her changed everything for Christy. God had given her a sign that she could have the marriage of her dreams. She just needed to convince David that his fears about marrying a career woman were ill founded.

"You just wait," she said in a deliberately light, teasing tone. "After a year you're not going to be able to let me go."

He smiled. "I guess anything is possible."

David Warner might think he had all the answers, but Christy knew they'd barely started exploring the questions. She knew he was scared, but in time she could overcome his fears. Finding a solution to their problems wasn't going to be easy, but God had never promised the road would be without stones.

Agnes had traveled a rocky road at the beginning of her marriage, but she'd held tight to her faith and her belief that God would never forsake her, and her marriage had weathered the storms of life. Deep in her heart Christy knew that despite his doubts, she and David could make it, too. All she had to do was remember that, with God's help, anything was possible.

Chapter Eleven

Christy finished reading the fifth chapter of Proverbs and closed her Bible. A few minutes earlier the grandfather clock in the hall had chimed eleven and David had kissed her on the cheek and gone up to his room. Alone.

On the surface, nothing had changed since their discussion earlier in the evening. They'd finished their meal and she'd helped him clear the table and fill the dishwasher. After that he'd read the paper while she reviewed a seminar she'd be giving in Kansas City next month.

The topic of the seminar was, appropriately, "love." The talk centered around the four different words used in New Testament Greek for love.

Though the topic was one of her favorites, it had

been hard for her to stay focused. The spicy scent of David's cologne had wafted about the room and sent her senses into overdrive. She didn't think he'd ever looked more handsome than he'd looked tonight and every time their gazes met, a shiver traveled up her spine.

He loves me.

She couldn't keep the words from running through her head. In all these years, he'd never stopped loving her. Surely a love that strong was capable of anything.

That brought her to "The Plan." It was foolproof. All she had to do was pull out all the stops. She'd take her seminar topic suggestions for strengthening a marriage and put them into action. By the end of the year he wouldn't be able to even think of letting her go.

"The Plan" would start tonight. She'd climb those stairs to his bed and she'd show him in no uncertain terms what he meant to her.

David stared at the ceiling. Though every fiber in his body ached for sleep, he was as wide-awake now as when he'd first climbed between the sheets thirty minutes ago.

Every time he closed his eyes, Christy's face flashed before him. Would he ever love another woman as much as he loved her? It seemed impossible. Unfortunately the very qualities he admired most in her—her determination, her drive and her compassion—were the same attributes that made him know she wouldn't be happy as a stay-at-home wife and mother.

He forced himself to think of the children he'd have someday. How could he condemn them to the life he'd had growing up—a lonely life with a father who worked long hours and a mother who was never home? But why was it so hard to imagine a child of his without Christy's blue eyes or bright smile?

Still, he couldn't compromise. They both deserved to be happy.

But how are you going to be happy without her?

David shoved the thought aside. It was a given that he'd miss her. Even tonight he'd waited to start dinner until right before she'd be home in hopes that she'd eat with him. He was playing with fire, but David couldn't keep his distance. They had only a year and he wanted to savor every moment.

''David?''

For a second he didn't move, convinced the soft, sweet voice was all in his imagination. Until he smelled the musky scent of her perfume.

He propped himself up on his elbows and stared. Though the room was dark, the mellow glow from a streetlight shining through the window bathed her slender form in a golden light.

She'd changed from her navy suit into a short, filmy chemise. Her blond hair hung loose to her shoulders. She looked like an angel.

"What are you doing here?" His voice came out in a raspy croak.

She smiled. "I thought we might talk."

"Talk?" This time the croak sounded more like a squeak. He cleared his throat and tried again. "What about?"

Christy didn't answer. Instead she crossed the room and settled gracefully on the bed next to him.

David forced his gaze to her face.

"I want to talk about this friendship thing." She ran a fingernail along his jaw, and the muscle tensed beneath her touch. "I've been thinking more about it, and though I like being friends I can't see why we should deprive ourselves of other pleasures during this next year."

"You want us to still sleep together?" His heart picked up speed.

"Sleeping?" She leaned over and brushed her lips against his. "I want you awake."

David's mind raced. Was he dreaming? And if not, would they only be hurt more by sharing this closeness? He sat up, taking in the sight and smell of her, and made his decision.

"Are you sure?" He gently fingered one of the tiny lace straps of her chemise.

"Positive." She smiled.

He returned her smile and hooked the strap with his finger. Slowly he pulled it down off her shoulder. Her smile widened.

David's heart pounded in his chest and his hand trembled as he swept the other strap off her shoulder.

"David." Her voice came out in a tremulous whisper.

"I want to make love to you," he said.

"Well, then, what are you waiting for?" Her eyes darkened with an unreadable emotion, but her voice was low and teasing. "We don't have all day."

"No." His hand moved to her waist and he pulled her to him. "But we do have all night."

Her lips met his and suddenly all night didn't seem long enough.

Chapter Twelve

By the time David stumbled half-asleep into the kitchen at seven-thirty, Christy had read her devotions, finished her workout and was ready for another cup of coffee.

"Care to join me?" She lifted the carafe.

He plopped down into the kitchen chair and laid his head on his folded arms.

"I need something," he said. "I feel like I've been hit by a Mack truck."

"I'll take that as a yes." Christy hid a smile and poured him a large mug of her favorite Colombian blend. She set the cup on the table in front of him and resisted the urge to smooth his hair. "Why are you so tired?"

He straightened with a groan. "As if you don't know."

Christy thought back to their night together and chuckled. "I guess some of us just have more stamina than others."

"Stamina?" He turned his head and met her gaze, all trace of sleepiness gone. The gleam in his eyes sent a shiver of anticipation coursing up her spine.

"I'll show you who's got stamina." In an instant David was on his feet and she was in his arms.

Christy's heart thudded in her chest as his mouth closed over hers. She returned his kiss with reckless abandon.

"Oh, Chrissy," he said in a ragged voice. "What you do to me."

What she did to him?

Christy drew a shuddering breath and brushed back the hair from her face with a trembling hand.

"You kiss me like that one more time," he said, "and I might have to call in sick and spend the day here."

"I think you'd be lonely here all by yourself," Christy said.

"But I wouldn't be alone," he said with an impish grin. "You'd be with me."

Christy couldn't help but smile at the thought. "I'd give you lots of TLC."

His eyes darkened for a moment. Then he shook

his head as if trying to clear the image from his thoughts.

"It is so incredibly tempting." He captured her hand with his and pressed a kiss into her palm. "But unfortunately Grandfather scheduled a meeting this morning with the board."

"Your loss." Christy shoved aside her disappointment and flashed him a bright smile. "It could have been one fun day."

"Keep that thought." David's dimple flashed. "Because one of these days it's going to happen."

"One of these days?" Christy rolled her eyes and dropped into a nearby chair. "When do you *ever* have a free day?"

"I could ask you the same thing." He took a seat opposite her.

"You're right," she said with a resigned sigh. "It was a good thought."

"Don't lose faith. It can happen," he said.

She wondered if he was trying to convince her or himself.

"We'll just have to schedule a time," he said.

"Schedule a sick day?" Christy said lifting a brow.

"Why not?"

"Okay, I'll pencil you in." She kept her tone light and offhand, not sure if he was serious or joking. Her gaze drifted to the clock. "But for now both of us better get moving."

Surprisingly, David didn't seem to be in any hurry. He lifted the cup to his lips and took a leisurely sip. "What's on the agenda for you today?"

"This morning I'm going to answer some e-mail, then I'm heading over to Sara's for Bible study," Christy said. "After lunch Tom is flying in from Chicago and we're going to go over some upcoming promotional events he has planned."

"Couldn't you do that over the phone?"

"We could," Christy said. "But I think he's really coming to see his sister in Winfield. He's driving there tomorrow to spend the day with her."

"What's he doing tonight?" David asked. "Does he have dinner plans? It might be nice if we took him out."

"Would you have time?" Christy asked, surprised at the offer.

"I could fit it in," David said. "If you want me to go, that is."

"I'd love it." Christy could hardly keep the eagerness from her voice. "I'll talk to Tom and give you a call at work. What time will you be out of your meeting?"

"Right now it's scheduled from nine to noon." David glanced at the clock on the wall and sprang to his feet. "I'd better get going."

David grabbed a piece of banana bread from the table and slathered it with butter before heading for the door.

"Call and let me know what's going on tonight," he said over his shoulder.

"Will you be home after work?"

David stopped and turned. He paused for a second. "I'm not sure how the afternoon will go. I'd better just plan on meeting you."

Christy shrugged. "Okay."

She expected him to head up the stairs immediately. After all, he still had to shower and get dressed. But he stood, shifting from one foot to another.

"Christy."

She raised a brow.

"I had a really good time last night," he said. "It was great."

Last night had gone way beyond making love. She and David had connected emotionally.

"I had a good time, too," she said softly.

Her heart turned over at the smile he flashed her.

"Get going, mister," she said, wanting nothing more than to be back in his arms. "I don't want you to be late."

He headed up the stairs and Christy leaned back in the chair, a broad smile on her face.

Yes, last night was definitely a step in the right direction, and she couldn't be more pleased.

Christy rang Sara's doorbell, eager anticipation coursing up her spine. In Chicago she'd been part of a Bible study group that met every week. She'd missed the Christian fellowship that was such an integral part of these sessions. And she'd missed the girl talk.

The second chime sounded and the door opened. Sara stood in the doorway, smiling a warm welcome. "Hi, Christy. I'm glad you could make it."

Sara ushered her down the hall to the great room and introduced her to several women who'd already arrived. She'd barely finished the introductions before the doorbell rang again.

"Christy, come and sit by me." Nancy, from the coffee shop, smiled and patted an empty spot beside her on the sofa.

Christy crossed the room and took the seat, returning Nancy's smile. "Looks like Sara is going to get a good turnout."

"She's expecting at least ten."

"Is that how many usually come?"

Nancy thought for a moment, then shrugged. "It's hard to say. We're a relatively new group. There have been as many as fifteen and as few as six show up."

"Can I get you ladies something to drink?" Sara returned to the room, looking more like a fashion model than a Bible study hostess in her black Nicole Miller skirt and custom-made shirt. "Lemonade? Iced tea? Soda?"

"Lemonade," Christy and Nancy said together.

"Great minds think alike," Nancy said with a smile.

"Exactly."

"I told my husband we'd met," Nancy said. "He thought it would be nice if we had you and David over for dinner some night."

"I'd like that," Christy said. A sense of satisfaction flowed through her like warm honey. They were starting to be viewed as a couple.

"Nancy, I'm sorry I'm late." Lauren hurried across the room, her gaze focused on the woman at Christy's side. "Did you save me a seat?"

Nancy shook her head. "I'm sorry. I didn't think you were coming."

Neither did I, thought Christy.

Sara had told Christy up front that Lauren came to Bible study only sporadically, when her work schedule allowed. Though she hadn't expected her today, Christy had accepted the fact that she and Lauren were now in the same social circle and that she'd better get used to seeing her.

"I can move," Christy said. "It's no problem at all."

"Don't worry about it." Lauren waved a dismissive hand. "There's an empty chair by Tina. I'll go sit over there."

Lauren shifted her gaze to Christy, surprising her with a slight smile. "I haven't seen you since Sara's party."

"It has been quite a while," Christy said, thinking it hadn't been nearly long enough. "By the way, happy birthday. Did you have a nice party?"

"David told you about it?" Lauren's gaze widened in mock surprise.

"Why shouldn't he?" Christy asked.

"I was surprised he didn't bring you along," Lauren said. "I asked him to."

Christy didn't believe for a moment that she'd been invited, but she forced a smile and decided to play along. "I'm afraid it didn't work out for me."

"It's time to get started. Everyone." Sara's voice sounded above the conversational chatter. "Could you all take your seats, please?"

Lauren smiled and headed across the room to the empty chair.

The dark-haired woman who greeted Lauren with a broad smile looked vaguely familiar, but Christy couldn't place her.

"Who is that woman to the right of Lauren?" she whispered in Nancy's ear.

Nancy shifted her gaze and replied in a low voice. "That's Tina Getz. She's Karen's sister."

"Karen?" Christy's voice rose in surprise. "Blake's wife?"

"That's the one," Nancy said. "Don't you think they look alike?"

Christy's gaze returned to the woman. Now that Nancy mentioned it, she could see the resemblance. Christy would have liked to ask Nancy more questions, but Sara clapped her hands.

"This week we're going to focus on specific pieces of text in James and Ephesians that deal with 'taming our tongue' and 'ridding ourselves of unwholesome talk.' Please open your Bibles to James, chapter three."

Christy pulled her Bible out of her bag and soon found herself immersed in God's word. Sara led the discussion with ease and by the final prayer Christy knew she'd found the group for her.

After the session she hung back and waited until Sara was alone.

"Thank you so much for inviting me." Christy gave Sara a quick hug.

"I'm just glad you could come," Sara said. "Did I tell you the next meeting is at your house?"

Momentarily speechless, Christy could only

stare. She tried to remember if she was even going to be in town next week.

Sara laughed. "I'm just kidding. You won't pop up on the rotation list for another month or so."

"That'll be fine," Christy said. "I'd love to have it at my house."

Only after the words left her mouth did Christy realize what she'd said. Sometime in the past few months she'd started thinking of David's house as her home. The thought made her smile widen.

"Are you headed home now?"

"I have some errands to run, then I have to meet with my publicist." Christy reached for her purse to take out her keys and realized she didn't have her bag. "But without my purse, I don't think I'm going anywhere."

Sara's brow furrowed. "You lost your purse?"

"No," Christy said with a wry grin. "It's around here somewhere. Actually, I think I left it in the other room."

"I'll get it for you," Sara said.

"You take care of your guests." Christy stopped her with a hand on her arm. "I think I know just where it is."

She hurried past two women standing in the foyer discussing the Bible topic. They smiled at her before resuming their conversation.

Christy had thought the room would be cleared

out, but when she got closer she realized that a few women must have stayed behind to talk.

"I'm telling you, it's the truth." The voice had a slight lisp and Christy immediately knew the speaker was Karen's sister Tina. She'd noticed the lisp when they were introduced during a refreshment break.

"How do you know?"

Although the second voice was soft and low, Christy recognized it, too. *Lauren.*

Christy stifled a groan. She'd had about all the polite conversation with her old friend that she could take in one day.

"Because her cleaning lady, Suzanne, told Karen's cleaning lady."

Suzanne? David's cleaning lady was named Suzanne. Christy's steps slowed even as her heart picked up speed.

"And she said they don't sleep in the same bedroom?" Lauren's voice was skeptical. "Are you sure?"

Christy's hand clenched at her side and her nails dug into her palm.

"Positive," Tina said. "What kind—"

"Excuse me." Christy walked into the room, her head held high, hoping the color she knew had to be in her cheeks gave nothing away. She retrieved her bag from the floor by the sofa. "I forgot my purse."

"We were just talking about the Scripture reading," Tina said with a phony smile.

Christy wanted to slap her.

Lauren shifted her gaze and said nothing.

"It was an interesting lesson," Christy said pointedly. "Especially that bit about taming our tongue. Don't you agree?"

Tina and Lauren looked at each other before they nodded.

Christy headed for the doorway. Though she'd have liked to tell them what she thought of their gossipy ways, she had more important matters to attend to.

She had a cleaning lady to fire.

"Do you mind if I have the last one?" Christy eyed the asparagus spring roll with unabashed interest. It didn't get much better than pasta, asparagus, cream cheese and smoked salmon all in one nice little roll. Though her entrée of beef tenderloin with peppercorns should be arriving any minute, it was almost eight o'clock and she was hungry *now*.

David shrugged his shoulders. "Fine with me."

Christy shifted her gaze to her publicist. Though she wanted nothing more than to snatch the appetizer from the plate, Tom was technically her guest and deserved first shot at it.

A smile creased Tom's lips. "It's all yours."

She flashed him a brilliant smile and lifted the tiny rolled lasagna noodle from the serving dish to her plate.

"You seem to have quite the appetite." Tom's gaze was filled with something akin to awe. "I don't remember you eating this much in Chicago."

"The air is fresher here," Christy said. "Besides, I haven't had that much, just a couple of—"

"Four," Tom said. "You've eaten half the plate. David had two. I had two. You had the rest."

She narrowed her gaze and dabbed at the corners of her mouth with the linen napkin.

"Not that I'm counting or anything," Tom said.

David's gaze shifted silently from her to Tom, but he didn't utter a word.

"David likes it when I eat," she said, deliberately taking a bite of the roll.

Tom laughed. "Yeah, but he's not the one who has to be concerned about you not fitting into all those clothes you bought last year."

Christy groaned. Tom had been on his "image" kick last year. He'd hired consultants to analyze all facets of her personal "image." The result was a couple of new lipstick colors and a more conservative group of suits designed to project an "aura of authority."

"Those suits fit as well as the day I got them," Christy said, deliberately ignoring the fact that the waistband of the one she'd worn yesterday had pinched a little. "You worry too much."

"Isn't that what you pay me to do?" Tom took a sip of the wine he'd ordered. He gestured to a bottle sitting tableside in a silver ice bucket. "Are you sure you won't join me?"

Christy's gaze met David's and his lips twitched. He was no doubt thinking that the last time they'd shared a bottle of wine they'd ended up married.

"I'll pass," David said.

"None for me, thanks." Christy's gaze shifted to the waiter heading toward them, a full tray balanced in one hand. "It looks like our food is here."

Over dinner Tom entertained David with stories about Christy's various faux pas during her presentations. Never being one to take herself too seriously, Christy laughed along with them. It had been a long time since she'd had such a pleasant meal.

She was grateful she was able to finish her crème brûlée before Tom steered the conversation back to work.

"I'm telling you now, next year is going to be

better than this one," Tom said. "The number of offers I have on my desk at this moment are up thirty percent over last year. And they're still coming in."

"Do you think that's because Christy is now married?" David asked.

"It certainly didn't hurt," Tom said. "To move into that top tier of motivational speakers she almost had to be married. No matter how knowledgeable, a single person talking about marriage just doesn't have the credibility that a married person does."

"But what about all the psychologists who go on television talking about raising children, who don't have any themselves?" David asked.

"I've never said it absolutely can't be done," Tom said. "Just that it's less likely to happen."

"Thirty percent more travel is a lot," David said. His gaze shifted to Christy. "Sounds like you're going to be racking up those frequent-flyer miles."

"If I accept all the offers." Christy met her husband's gaze. "Just because some group asks me to come doesn't mean I will."

"Of course not," Tom said. "There's a lot to consider—size of the group, type of group, topic they want presented—"

"Location and how long I'd be out of town," Christy interjected.

Tom looked at her for a moment. "That, too, I guess."

"I guess I should congratulate you," David said in a hearty voice that sounded forced to her ears. "It looks like your career is headed straight for the stars."

She reached under the table and squeezed his hand. For a moment she thought he was going to pull away, but then his fingers laced though hers.

It will work out, she promised herself. David loved her and she loved him. How could it not?

"Don't you just love opera?" Karen smiled up at her husband and wrapped her arm though his.

Blake saw little choice but to return his wife's smile. Actually he hated opera. And he especially disliked *Tosca,* the one he'd been forced to sit through this evening. But he did like mingling with the cream of St. Louis society at these events, and if it made his wife happy in the bargain, that was an extra bonus.

"I've had a nice evening," Blake said smoothly, thinking specifically of the two business contacts he'd made during intermission.

"I'm glad." She squeezed his arm. "It's too bad David and Christy couldn't go with us."

"Yes, it is." Blake would have liked having his cousin suffer through the opera with him.

They exited the Opera Theatre and instead of keeping up with the crowd heading for a nearby parking garage, Karen slowed her steps. "Blake, we need to talk."

"I thought that's what we were doing," he said, narrowing his gaze. Was that the mayor up ahead in the tan topcoat?

"I've got something to tell you."

The tan topcoat got into a black Lincoln parked in a no-parking area, and Blake shifted his gaze to his wife.

She looked so serious. What could she possibly have to tell him that they hadn't already discussed? Karen had little interest in anything beyond him, their home and the children.

Could it be something with the girls? They'd looked okay when he'd seen them briefly before he and Karen had left for dinner. She'd been fussing over them as if they were leaving for days instead of just going out for the evening. But then, she always had babied them.

A cold chill ran down Blake's spine and he shifted his gaze to the woman beside him. Was it his imagination or had she seemed a little too happy lately? Could she have pulled a fast one on him?

"Don't tell me you're pregnant?"

"Goodness, no." A look of surprise crossed her face and she laughed.

Blake breathed a sigh of relief and let his mind wander while Karen jabbered on about the merits of having more children. She didn't stop talking about babies until they were in the Lexus and out of the parking garage.

"How did we ever start talking about babies?" she asked, buckling her seat belt.

"You said you had something to tell me." Blake edged the car onto the freeway.

"That's right," she said with a little laugh. "How did we get so off track?"

Blake didn't want to go down that road again. He ignored the question and raised a brow. "Your news?"

"David fired his cleaning lady." A tiny frown furrowed Karen's brow. "Or maybe Christy did. I don't know for sure."

Blake's hands tightened around the steering wheel and an expletive slipped past his lips.

"I knew you'd be upset," his wife said. "That's why I didn't tell you earlier. I feel so bad for the woman."

Blake's gaze shot to his wife.

"You don't think it's because Christy and David found out she'd been talking, do you?" she said.

"How could they?" Blake said. "I didn't say anything to anyone. Did you?"

"Only to my sister." Karen's gaze shifted to her hands. "It just slipped out one day when we were talking. But Tina promised she wouldn't say anything."

Tina Getz had never kept a secret in her life. Blake doubted if the woman even knew what the word meant. But it didn't matter why the cleaning lady had left, or who had done the firing. The only thing that mattered was his only link to the inner workings of his cousin's household was gone.

Now he had to figure out what he was going to do about it.

Chapter Thirteen

David's grandfather walked to his office door and pulled it until it clicked shut before returning to the high-backed leather desk chair. Though the meeting with the board of directors earlier in the week had gone off without a hitch, David shifted uneasily in his seat. His grandfather's request for some of his time this morning had taken him by surprise. The older man had to know that an unscheduled meeting would throw David's whole day into disarray. Therefore something big had to be up.

"I suppose you're wondering what this is all about?" His grandfather leaned back in his chair and studied David.

"A little," David said, knowing his grandfather expected honesty. "Does it have to do with the board meeting?"

"In a way." The older man paused and his expression turned serious. "Remember when Harvey Jacques asked me if I would be willing to stay on the board in an advisory capacity?"

"Was that during the break?" David asked, the memory hazy at best.

His grandfather nodded. "Do you recall my answer?"

David thought for a moment, then shook his head. "I'm sorry, I don't. But you said yes, didn't you?"

"Actually I told Harv that I'd have to think about it."

"Think about it?" David frowned. "What is there to think about?"

"I said that just to buy some time." The older man met David's gaze. "I plan to say no, but I needed to talk to you first."

"You're going to say no? But why?" A tightness gripped David's chest. "You're not sick, are you?"

"I'm healthy as a horse and rarin' to get on with my life." His grandfather chuckled. "David, Lorraine Keller has consented to be my wife. We plan to be married in October, then after our honeymoon we'll be moving to Phoenix."

"You're marrying Mrs. Keller?" David couldn't hide his shock. He knew his grandfather and the spry widow had attended various social events together over the past year, but he'd never dreamed it was more than friendship. He couldn't imagine his grandfather married to anyone but his grandmother. "But she was Grandma's friend."

"That's right. And her husband was mine. But Myra and John are both gone now. I love Lorraine. And she loves me. Your grandmother and John would have wanted us to be happy."

"I want you to be happy, too," David said. He knew how lonely his grandfather had been since his grandmother had died. "But why Phoenix?"

"Lorraine's daughters live in Scottsdale," he said. "And her grandson is in Tucson. But we're only going to winter down there. That way I can be close to my family part of the year and she can be close to hers."

"Sounds like you've got it all figured out," David said. He paused for a moment. "Is this why you were in such a hurry for me to take over the company?"

His grandfather's smile turned sheepish. "Lorraine and I hadn't made any firm plans then, but I could see where our relationship was headed. I didn't want to be tied to work."

"But your father started the business." David couldn't believe the lack of regret in his grandfather's voice. "You don't even sound like you're going to miss it."

"I don't think I will."

"But how can you walk away from something that's been your whole life for sixty years?"

His grandfather shook his head. "You've got it all wrong, David. I love the company and I'm proud of the men and women who work for us and proud of the products we produce, but the business has never been my whole life. Your grandmother, my family, my faith, that's what gave my life meaning."

"But Warner Enterprises is your legacy—"

"David." His grandfather leaned forward and pinned David with his gaze. "Things of this earth are only temporary. In the grand scheme of things, they aren't important."

"So you're saying it doesn't matter if the company makes a profit or not? Or whether our employees continue to have a job or not?" David threw up his hands in frustration. "Maybe we should have just let Blake sell it off piece by piece."

"Blake and I had a long talk yesterday. He realizes now that dismantling the company would have been a shortsighted move."

David couldn't believe his ears. Normally his grandfather could see through a snow job, but

Blake had obviously conned the old man. David raked his fingers through his hair. When he'd come to work that morning it had seemed like a normal day. Now nothing made sense. "Tell me something. Why did you tie my taking over the company to being married?"

"I already told you," his grandfather said. "I believe this company needs a family man at its helm."

"That doesn't make any sense," David said. "A single man would have more time to devote to the job."

"You're right. It doesn't make much sense when you think of it that way," his grandfather admitted. "But let me try to explain it another way. I want more for you than success in business. I want you to have a full, rich life like the one your grandmother and I shared. I was afraid if you were single when you took over, you'd stay that way. You'd be so into proving yourself, you wouldn't have time to build a relationship. The years would pass and one day you'd look around and discover that you were all alone."

"Now I *am* married," David said. "And I barely have time to give my wife the time of day."

"Don't blame anybody or anything other than yourself if that's the case." His grandfather shot David a stern look. "If you're not making time for her, then you need to look at your priorities. You made a promise to God that you would love, honor and cherish that young woman and if you're slighting her, you're not fulfilling your part of the bargain.''

''But...'' A thousand valid excuses rose to David's lips.

''Son.'' His grandfather spoke sharply. ''We make time for what is important to us. If Christy and your marriage are important to you, you'll do whatever it takes to find the time to make it work.''

David swallowed the words of protest. He could see by his grandfather's firm expression that the old man's mind was made up. No excuse, no reason, would be good enough.

And David wasn't so sure he would be that effective arguing with his grandfather. The censuring words had hit their mark. And at this moment he wasn't sure he disagreed with them.

The rest of the day David couldn't think of anything else. When five o'clock rolled around, David locked up his office and headed home, anxious to see Christy and tell her there would soon be another wedding in the family.

Lights shone in the kitchen and he smiled as he pushed open the door, anticipating her reaction to the news. ''Christy—''

He stopped. A single place was set at the table

and a piece of bright-yellow paper rested on top of the china plate.

Disappointment rushed through David like a raging river. He moved to the table, snatched up the paper and quickly read the note.

David,
Pastor called, and the woman who was supposed to be in the church nursery this evening is sick. I agreed to fill in.
There's leftover spaghetti in the fridge.
Be home around ten.
Love, Christy

David crumpled the note in one hand. He glanced at his watch, then down at the briefcase full of work. Without any distractions he could make a good dent in his paperwork. Or he could surprise Christy and keep her company at the church.

For an instant David thought about tossing a coin, but he decided it would just be a waste of time. He already knew what he wanted to do.

He set his briefcase on the table and headed for the door.

Tucked into a far corner of the church basement, the church nursery was a small room that had recently been redecorated. The old knotty-pine paneling had been replaced with drywall and the floor tile had been covered with a textured carpet. David barely noticed the changes. He had eyes only for the antique oak rocking chair in one corner.

Oblivious to his presence in the doorway, Christy rocked back and forth in the ornate chair. A tiny dark-haired baby wrapped in a blue blanket was cradled in her arms while two toddlers played at her feet.

Christy had dressed casually for the evening in jeans and a fuzzy green sweater. Her long hair was pulled back into a ponytail and she'd exchanged the hoop earrings she normally wore for tiny studs.

Obviously she knew little children, David thought with a wry grin. He remembered Blake's daughters when they were small. Their hands seemed to be constantly searching for something to grab or pull.

These children seemed remarkably subdued. The room was quiet except for a soft lullaby coming from Christy's lips. The tune was one his grandmother used to sing to him when he'd been a little boy.

For a second an image of Christy holding his son—their son—flashed before him. His heart clenched. How could something seem so right and so wrong at the same time?

"David?"

His head jerked up.

"What are you doing here?" Christy's voice was so soft she almost whispered the words.

"I thought—"

She pressed her fingers to her lips and he lowered his voice.

"I thought I'd keep you company," he said, speaking in the same hushed tones she'd used. "If that's okay?"

"Of course it's okay." Her pleased smile warmed his heart. "I'm glad to have you here."

David took a seat on an overstuffed sofa. The toddlers looked up briefly at the movement before turning back to their toys.

"What's going on tonight?" David had barely glanced at the church's weekly events calendar last Sunday. "There weren't many cars in the lot."

"Pastor and his wife are conducting a class for single parents." Christy repositioned the sleeping baby in her arms. "Apparently they meet once a month. Though they have a topic to discuss, the main purpose is Christian fellowship and support."

"Being a single parent would be hard," David said. "I can see where they'd need the support."

"Babies demand a lot of time," Christy said. She stroked the baby's shiny black hair. "But they're worth it."

David stared. Christy seemed so at ease in this role. He'd never thought of her as being a baby person. "I was surprised you agreed to help out in the nursery."

"Why would you be surprised?"

"I don't know." David shrugged. "I guess I would have pictured you upstairs leading tonight's discussion rather than down here changing diapers."

"I like children," Christy said simply. "When I was growing up my sister and I baby-sat all the time."

"Still, wouldn't you rather—"

"David." She cut him off, as if she knew just where he was headed. "I like variety in my life. I work with big people every day." Her gaze dropped to the little girl with red curls at her feet and her smile softened. "This gives me the opportunity to be with the little ones for a change."

How could he have forgotten her kind heart? She'd been that way even as a teen. And now here she was, ten years later, cuddling another woman's baby to her chest as tenderly as if the little boy were her own.

Could such a woman ever neglect her own child? He couldn't imagine it. A tiny of flicker of hope rose inside him. For the first time he let himself believe, for just a moment, that this marriage could work, and that he really could have it all.

David dropped an extra handful of marshmallows into the hot cocoa. Although Christy had fallen asleep as soon as her head hit the pillow, sleep had eluded him.

Ever since he'd stopped by the nursery, his mind had been a jumble of confusing thoughts and emotions. Could he and Christy make this marriage work?

She'd said a child needed both parents. Thinking back to his own childhood, David had to admit that though his father rarely traveled, he hadn't been that available. His dad had been an old-fashioned guy who'd believed a man's job was to work and a woman's job was to take care of the home and her family. When his wife didn't quite fit that mold, instead of compromising, his father did nothing but blame her.

Bits and pieces of long-forgotten memories nudged at the edge of David's consciousness. His mother rearranging a business trip so she could be in town for his soccer game. Funny little notes left on the top of the casseroles she'd made up for her family when she was out of town. Would he have thought much about her business trips if his father hadn't always been pointing out how neglected they were?

David knew his parents had loved each other in their own way. He often wondered—if their lives hadn't been cut short in a car accident three years ago, would they have found some measure of peace in their later years?

David set the mug of cocoa on the table and wiped his eyes with the back of his hand.

Christy had filled the void in his life that had been there since his parents had died. His house felt like a home again. At the end of the day he found himself looking forward to coming home. And that anticipation didn't have one thing to do with a hot meal on the table or a clean house. It had to do with the fact that Christy was there, waiting for him.

God hadn't given him the type of woman he'd asked for in his prayers, but He'd given him the woman he needed to make his life complete.

Christy had been right all along. They *could* work this out. After all, with God's help, anything was possible.

Christy stared at David out of the corner of her eye and picked up her pace.

It was still hard to believe that the handsome man running at her side was her husband.

Since that night in the church, something had changed. She couldn't quite put her finger on it, but David had been more relaxed, more loving lately. A couple of times she'd wanted to ask him if he still thought of their marriage as temporary, but she'd held back, not wanting to rush things.

"Want to go a little farther today?" They were nearing the end of their normal five-mile route and almost home, but after trying on a skirt she hadn't worn in a few months, she'd decided she'd better kick her exercise regime to the next level.

"How much farther?" David wiped a thin layer of sweat from his brow with the back of his hand.

"I don't know. Couple more miles. Maybe three," Christy said. "We can play it by ear."

"I'd like to," David said. "But I need to go into the office a little earlier than usual. We've got some consultants coming in from New York."

"I'll see you later, then," Christy said. "Go ahead and lock the door when you leave. I have a key with me."

"Don't you think five miles is enough?"

"Normally, yes," Christy said. "But I tried on one of the 'power' suits Tom insisted I buy last year and instead of looking polished and professional I looked like Petunia Pig. So it's less food and more exercise for this girl."

David eased his pace down a notch and Christy slowed her gait momentarily to match his.

"You're beautiful, Christy," he said, his gaze firm and direct. "Don't let Tom tell you differently. I like you just the way you are."

"Thank you." Her heart warmed at the sincerity in his tone. "Unfortunately, Tom won't see it the same way. He's got some big things in the works and you know how he is about projecting a certain image."

The turnoff to their street loomed ahead and it took all of Christy's willpower not to change her mind and follow David. Instead she gave him a wave and a smile and picked up the pace.

Unwavering dedication to her goals had served her well in the past. She could demand nothing less of herself now.

Chapter Fourteen

"Mr. Warner?"

David lifted his gaze from the computer screen. His administrative assistant stood in the doorway to his office, her normally cheerful face serious.

"I'd like to leave a couple of hours early tomorrow. If that's okay with you, that is." Joni's words came out in a rush.

David lifted a brow. "Caleb have another field trip?"

Joni didn't have a lot of vacation built up and lately all her requests for time off had been to attend her son's school events or to accompany him and his classmates on various outings.

"Not this time." Joni smiled. "This is for me. I've been thinking. Getting off at five only gives me a few hours to get ready for the gala. I need some breathing room. I don't want to have to rush.''

The gala started at eight, which to David seemed like more than enough time for anyone to shower and pull on some clothes. But it was Joni's vacation time and he didn't have to approve the reason, only the time off. Normally he'd have said yes without a second thought. But the Granger proposal had to be ready to go by Monday. Joni hadn't even begun to add the graphics to his written report.

David hesitated, trying to think if he had any other staff that could pitch in and help. He couldn't think of a single person.

Joni's gaze searched his, and for an instant he had the uncanny feeling she could read his mind.

''If it's about that proposal, I could take it home this weekend,'' Joni said. ''Or come in and do it.''

David thought for a moment. ''If you want to do that, you can forget about taking vacation time. We can just exchange hours.''

''Sounds good to me.'' Joni grinned. ''Caleb's dad will have him this weekend, so I'll have plenty of time to work on those graphics.''

''We have a deal,'' David said. ''Leave whenever you want tomorrow.''

"Thanks, Mr. Warner." Joni flashed him a bright smile and pulled the door shut behind her.

David sat back in his chair and glanced at the clock. A little over an hour remained until his next meeting. Barely enough time to run out for a quick sandwich. He picked up the phone intending to call Christy and see if she was up for some quick Chinese-to-go when he remembered that Tom was back in town.

David heaved a disappointed sigh, hung up the phone and shifted his attention back to the computer screen. Rows of endless numbers had him rubbing the bridge of his nose in a matter of minutes.

Always more of a people person, David loved meeting with clients, finding out their needs and convincing them Warner Enterprises was the company for them. But since he'd taken over as CEO, the focus of his job had shifted to reports and meetings.

If he were a paper pusher like Blake, with a degree in accounting and a penchant for sitting behind a desk, he'd be set.

David wondered idly if Blake really had changed his mind and no longer favored dismantling the company. Though David hoped that was the case, he couldn't help but be skeptical. Blake was smart enough to say whatever it took to stay on the old man's good side.

"A penny for your thoughts."

David's gaze shot up at the familiar voice.

"Or maybe I should raise that amount." Lauren sauntered into the room, looking like a breath of spring in a yellow print dress. "Inflation, you know."

"Lauren, hello." David couldn't keep the surprise from his voice. Though she used to pop in and see him all the time, this was the first time since he'd gotten married that she'd stopped by. "I didn't expect to see you today. Have a seat."

She looked especially pretty today. Her green eyes sparkled and a rosy pink flushed her cheeks. The pale yellow of the dress accentuated her tan and the cut enhanced her soft curves. She sat down gracefully in the leather wing-back and crossed one long tan leg over the other.

"Joni was on her way out the door for a hot lunch date," Lauren said with a smile. "I told her I'd let myself in."

"I didn't even hear you."

"Making an entrance is my forte," Lauren said with an impudent grin. "Remember that time at the club?"

"Are you referring to the time you tripped on

the rug and took a waiter and a tray of drinks down with you?'' David laughed.

Lauren's laughter mingled with his. ''We've had some good times, haven't we?''

''Yes, we have.'' David couldn't dispute her words. They'd always had fun together. He and Lauren had been great friends and he liked her a lot. But being around Christy the past four months had made him realize the difference between liking someone and *loving* someone.

''What brings you down here today?'' David said. ''Shouldn't you be at work?''

Lauren taught kindergarten part-time at a private school and tutored several evenings a week.

''Broadview Academy is out for the summer,'' Lauren said with an understanding smile, and he knew she wasn't surprised he didn't remember. In all the years they'd dated, he'd never been able to keep her schedule straight. ''I came down here on the off chance that you were free. There's something I want to discuss with you.''

''I have about forty-five minutes,'' David said. ''How about if we go across the street to Conroy's and grab a quick lunch?''

''Sounds good to me,'' Lauren said. ''If you're sure Christy won't mind. I don't want to cause any trouble.''

Her hesitation caught him off guard. After all

these years and the closeness they'd shared, he hated the thought that she should feel so unsure.

"Of course, I have time. And Christy knows we're just friends." David flashed her a reassuring smile. "The only thing we have to worry about is whether we can get a table or not."

Thankfully, the restaurant across the street from the manufacturing plant wasn't as busy as usual and they were seated immediately. Located in an area heavily populated by industry, the mom-and-pop diner catered to its working-class neighbors. It was well-known for its wide range of stick-to-your-ribs kind of food.

David glanced around the dining room, remembering last Sunday when he and Christy had stopped there after church. "Christy loves coming here, especially for breakfast. She says they make the best oatmeal."

Lauren leaned back in the booth and a tiny smile played at the corners of her lips. "Well, I never thought I'd see the day."

"What?" David asked.

"You're in love." The smile still lingered on her lips, but a hint of sadness darkened her eyes.

"Of course I am," he said gruffly, feeling embarrassed but not sure why. "That's why people get married."

"I know." Lauren shifted her gaze, took a tall

glass of iced tea from the waitress and smiled her thanks. "But you have to admit the way you and Christy got married wasn't like most people."

"I don't know about that," David said, refusing to acknowledge the point he knew she was trying to make. "Lots of couples get married in Las Vegas."

"To someone they barely know?"

"We'd known each other." He couldn't quite keep the defensive edge from his voice.

"True. But you hadn't been dating her," Lauren said softly. "You'd been dating me. And I'm not the only one who wondered about this sudden marriage of yours. Most think you just gave in to your grandfather's pressure and made an impulsive mistake."

"Is that what you think my marriage is?" he said. "A mistake?"

"I did," she admitted grudgingly. "But I've been giving it a lot of thought lately and I don't feel that way anymore."

"I'm glad. Because no matter what anyone says or thinks, my marrying Christy wasn't a mistake." His voice shook with emotion.

David didn't care what people said about him, but he hated the thought of them saying anything about Christy. She deserved more than what she'd gotten so far—a rushed wedding in front of Elvis with no family or friends and no honeymoon. But he vowed he'd make it up to her, even if it took the next fifty years.

Fifty years.

A lifetime of love.

Till death do us part.

He realized suddenly that he wanted to spend the rest of his life with Christy. He wanted her to be his wife and the mother of his children.

"David?" Lauren reached across the table and touched his hand. "I didn't mean to offend you."

He clasped her hand and gave it a reassuring squeeze. "Don't worry about it."

His gaze met hers and he knew he had his own amends to make.

"I'm sorry I hurt you." The words came out in a rush. "Marrying Christy in Las Vegas may have been an impulsive decision, but it was the right one. What wasn't right was the fact that I never really considered how this would impact you. I mean, we'd talked about marriage only in the most general of terms, but still…"

"David." Lauren leaned forward, her green eyes large and luminous. "It was a shock. I won't pretend it wasn't. I mean, I honestly thought it would be me getting a diamond in Las Vegas. But we both deserve to be happy. And I realize now I never would be happy married to a man who doesn't love me.''

"You know I care for you, Lauren,'' David said.

"I know you do,'' she said. "But you don't love me. I want someone who does.''

"What about Rusty?'' David asked. "Have you thought about giving him a chance? He's always liked you.''

"I know,'' Lauren said with a sigh. Her gaze shifted to a point over David's left shoulder. "He's a great guy. A good friend. But there's no spark.''

"Maybe the spark is just slow to ignite.'' Even to David's ears, the argument sounded weak, but he owed it to Rusty to give it his best shot.

"If it's not there, it's not there,'' Lauren said, meeting his gaze. "You should know that.''

David shifted uncomfortably in his chair. All he could think of was Rusty and how devastated he would be to learn he didn't have a chance.

"What about tomorrow night?''

"The gala?'' Lauren raised a dark brow. "What about it?''

"Are you still going?''

"I'd planned on it.'' Her gaze narrowed. "Why? Do you think I shouldn't?''

"No, you need to go,'' David said quickly. "But some day soon you're going to have to let Rusty know the score. You can't lead him on.''

Lauren stared at David for a long moment. He shifted uncomfortably beneath her penetrating gaze. "I wouldn't think of doing that."

The waitress cleared her throat and David looked up to find her standing next to their table with two plates of food. She gestured to the table and David realized with a start that he still held Lauren's hand. David quickly released it and glanced around the dining area, hoping no one he knew had seen him. Thankfully he didn't recognize anyone in the dining room.

David breathed a sigh of relief, added some ketchup to his megaburger and changed the subject. "Got any big plans for this summer?"

"As a matter of fact, I do have some big plans. The news will leak out sooner or later, and I wanted you to be the first to know," Lauren said matter-of-factly. "I'm going to have a baby."

"You're pregnant?" David set the bottle of ketchup down on the table with a clatter and his voice boomed across the half-empty dining room. "But how can that be?"

At a small table nearby, half-hidden behind a large plastic tree, Tina Getz pricked up her ears. She'd seen David and Lauren walk in and she'd thought about strolling over to say hello. Instead she'd waited and watched. Now she was glad she had.

Who would have thought they'd have the nerve to hold hands in public? But they must have been doing a lot more than that in private for Lauren to turn up pregnant. Tina couldn't wait to break the news to Blake and Karen that David's old girlfriend was pregnant with his baby.

The only one that Tina felt sorry for in this whole sordid mess was Christy. Though she'd been introduced to David's wife just that one time, Tina could only imagine Christy's reaction when she found out what her husband had done.

Because it was a given that she'd find out. Tina couldn't be expected to keep this kind of information quiet, no sirree. By tomorrow night everyone would know what David Warner had been up to, including David's new bride.

Chapter Fifteen

***

"Didn't the baby-sitter tell you I'd called?" Tina brushed past Karen, not waiting for her sister to invite her in. "I stayed up until two waiting to hear from you."

"I didn't think you'd want to be awakened in the middle of the night," Karen said mildly.

"Do you have any coffee?" Tina asked abruptly.

"I just brewed a pot."

Without another word her sister headed for the kitchen, with Karen trailing after her. Tina made herself at home, grabbing a mug from the cupboard and filling it with coffee.

"You have any cream?" Tina asked.

Karen opened the refrigerator door and pulled out a carton of half-and-half.

"That'll do." Tina took it from her hands, added a dollop to her cup and took a big sip.

Karen poured herself a cup and took a seat at the table opposite her sister. "So are you going to tell me what's going on?"

"Oh, now you're interested?" Tina's eyes widened in mock surprise. "Last night you couldn't be bothered to pick up the phone."

Karen took a deep breath and counted to ten. "Like I said, we didn't get home until after midnight. If you'd said it was urgent, I would have called."

Tina took a long sip of coffee. "Okay, I guess I forgive you." Tina pulled out a chair and sat down, crossing one slender leg over the other. Her gaze narrowed. "Why aren't you dressed yet?"

Karen cinched the belt of her robe tight around her waist and resisted the urge to run her fingers through her disheveled hair. "Maybe because it's barely six-thirty and we just got up. Blake is still in the shower."

"I was at the gym at five-thirty," Tina said.

"Good for you," Karen said dryly, reaching for the pot of coffee. "Now, about this news of yours—"

"I thought I heard voices." Blake stood in the doorway, dressed in a navy suit, his hair still slightly damp.

"Tina and I were just gabbing," Karen said, shooting a glance at her sister. Tina hadn't said if her news was for Karen's ears only.

"Actually, I was just telling your wife I have some news." Tina refilled her coffee cup and smiled at Blake. "News about your cousin, David. I think you'll find it extremely interesting."

"Really?" Blake took a seat at the table and signaled for Karen to pour him a cup of coffee. "What is it?"

"David is going to be a daddy." Tina spoke slowly and deliberately, evenly spacing her words for maximum effect.

"Why, that's wonderful," Karen squealed. "I didn't know he and Christy had been thinking of starting a family just yet, but—"

"Karen," Tina said sharply. "Will you stop and listen for a minute?"

"By all means, tell us what you know," Blake said smoothly, taking a steaming mug of coffee from Karen's hands. "When is this blessed event supposed to occur? And how did you find out about it?"

"I overheard David and Lauren talking at Conroy's," Tina said.

"David and Lauren?" Karen stared at her sister. "Don't you mean David and Christy?"

"No." Tina's lips curved up in a Cheshire-cat grin. "I mean Lauren."

Blake sat up straight in his chair, his gaze riveted to Tina. "Are you saying what I think you're saying?"

"You're a smart guy, Blake," Tina cooed. "I knew you'd get it."

Karen's gaze shifted from her husband to her sister and a sense of unease coursed up her spine. "Well, I'm glad you two are on the same wavelength, because you've lost me."

Blake's lips tilted in a slight smile. He lifted his coffee cup and took a sip before answering. "It's really quite simple, my dear. Lauren is the one having David's baby, not Christy."

"Oh, no." Karen's hand rose to her throat. Her heart clenched as she imagined what Christy must be feeling.

This was horrible news. Simply horrible. But what Karen didn't understand was why, if Tina and Blake understood the situation, did they look so pleased?

Christy smiled at Tom. "I'm glad you're coming to the gala tonight."

"It's going to be great." Tom leaned back in the kitchen chair. "The *Post-Dispatch* is sending a reporter and a photographer. We should be able to get some good publicity out of it.''

She shot him an exasperated look. ''Is business all you think about?''

Tom shrugged. ''Yep.''

Christy's laughter filled the air. ''At least you're honest. What am I going to do with you?''

''Reward me monetarily.'' Tom gestured to the stack of speaking engagement requests piled on the table. ''Look at all the bookings I've brought in. And no need for any special thanks on those European dates.''

Christy wanted to tell him she hadn't said yes to confirming any of those dates yet, but she didn't have the heart. He was so pleased with himself.

After the gala, she and David would have time to talk. Then she'd decide what dates to accept. Though she wasn't particularly interested in doing the dates in France and Germany because of the amount of time she'd be away from home, it might work out if David could wrangle some time off and come with her. Since they'd never gone anywhere after they'd married, this could be a belated honeymoon.

Though she'd never thought of herself as a romantic, lately she'd found herself wishing she'd had a traditional wedding with the walk down the aisle on her father's arm and with family and friends gathered around to hear their vows. And it would have been nice to have a honeymoon, too.

"So are you ready to sign the contracts now?" Tom said, interrupting her daydream of David slathering suntan lotion on her bare back.

"Give me a few more days to look at the offers," she said. She raised a hand, effectively stopping his protests. "I'm sure they'll be fine, but right now I have too much on my mind to give them my full attention."

Tom's gaze searched her eyes. "Okay. We can probably hold off until next week. But tell me, what's more important than these offers?"

"I have to decide…" Christy paused for effect and forced her expression to stay serious. "Whether I should wear my hair up for the party—" she scooped her hair in one hand and twisted it up off her neck "—or down."

She released the long strands and let them tumble loosely around her shoulders. Christy batted her eyes and stared at her publicist. "What do you think?"

Tom rolled his eyes. "I think this marriage of yours has made you goofier than a fruit fly."

Christy laughed. Ever since she and David had resolved their differences, she'd found herself laughing for no reason. Tom was right. She was goofy. She was silly. But most of all she was happy. Happy that God had sent David to be part of her life.

She basked in the warmth of the emotions. How could it get much better than this?

Chapter Sixteen

David stood in the doorway of the hotel ballroom and gazed out over the sea of people. Seeing everyone dressed in their tuxedos and fancy gowns, he scarcely recognized the men and women he'd worked with for years.

His gaze shifted to the woman beside him. Resplendent in a black filmy concoction that accentuated her blond good looks, Christy seemed equally awed by the spectacle before them.

She smiled up at him. "Now I understand why you call it a gala."

He tightened his arm around her waist and sent a prayer of thanks heavenward. He was so lucky to have been given this second chance. Why had he wasted so much time focusing on why their marriage wouldn't work instead of just trusting in God that it would?

He impulsively leaned down and brushed a kiss across Christy's lips.

"What was that for?" Her face pinked with pleasure.

"Because I love you," he said.

"I love you, too," she said softly, reaching up to lightly touch his cheek with one hand. "Very much."

"Hey, you two." Rusty's amused voice was like a splash of cold water. "Break it up."

David held Christy's gaze for a moment longer before shifting his attention to his friend. He widened his eyes. "Rusty? Is that you?"

"He cleans up pretty nice, doesn't he?" Lauren said in a teasing tone from his side.

David had to agree. Instead of flying every which way, Rusty's hair had been trimmed and moussed into submission. The black tux showed off his lean, muscular build to full advantage. David hoped his friend didn't blow it now. Tonight was Rusty's last chance to impress Lauren.

"You look pretty nice yourself, Lauren." David gazed appreciatively at her. The dress she wore was a pale green, so light it was almost white. Though he wasn't a connoisseur of women's clothing, he'd been around enough to know that the fashionably cut dress hadn't come off a rack.

"Why, thank you." Lauren flashed him a smile. "How sweet of you to say so."

Rusty's smile faded and his arm slipped possessively around Lauren's shoulders. "Back off, buddy. She's mine."

David laughed as if Rusty were joking, though he had a sinking feeling his friend was serious.

"Actually—" Lauren stepped out from Rusty's arm "—I don't belong to anyone but myself."

The smile stayed on her face, but the warning in her tone was unmistakable.

David nearly groaned out loud. In his haste to stake his claim, Rusty had moved way too fast. If his friend didn't slow down, David had the feeling his friend might find himself out of the game before he'd even got up to bat.

"I didn't mean anything by it, honey," Rusty said, using the endearment as loosely as if this was their tenth date and not their first.

David shot his friend a warning glance.

"I know how close the two of you have been," Rusty continued, seemingly oblivious to the dangerous ground he was treading upon. "I just want you and David to remember that he's married now."

Christy tensed beside him.

David gritted his teeth. "I don't know what you're getting at, Rusty, but I take my wedding vows seriously."

"Rusty, I think it's time we danced." Lauren grabbed his arm and pulled him toward the dance floor.

David watched the two of them weave their way into the crowd before he turned back to Christy. He couldn't help but be embarrassed by his friend's behavior. "What do you think got into him?"

"I'd say too much beer," Christy said.

"Beer?" David frowned. Unlike some of their other friends, he and Rusty had never been much for alcohol. "What makes you think that?"

Christy's eyes reflected her surprise. "Didn't you smell it on him?"

"No," David said. "I didn't."

"I might be wrong," Christy said with a shrug.

"He was all tensed up about his date tonight," David mused. "I wonder if he thought the alcohol would relax him?"

"Maybe," Christy said, a thoughtful look in her eye. "But he better be careful or he's going to say or do something he regrets."

David wished he could help his friend, but it was up to Rusty now. He held out his hand. "I'm tired of talking about Rusty. What I'd like to do is to dance with my wife. Shall we?''

Christy tilted her head as if she had to think about it, but the twinkle in her eyes gave her away.

''I'd love to dance with you,'' she said, finally taking his hand.

When they reached the dance floor David pulled her close, the musky scent of her perfume teasing his nose. He inhaled deeply and lost himself in the music and the closeness.

His grandfather danced up beside them, his arms firmly around a radiant Lorraine. ''Having a good time?''

''Wonderful,'' David answered. He'd never meant anything more.

He danced with Christy for several more songs until she caught a glimpse of an old high school friend and excused herself to go over to say hello.

David saw Tom standing alone off to the side and realized that he'd been so into dancing with his wife that he'd barely said two words to Tom all evening.

David headed across the room, only to be way-laid by Karen's sister Tina. ''If you're looking for your girlfriend, she's over by the punch bowl.''

David frowned. ''Who?''

''You know very well who I'm talking about,''

Tina chided. "Sexy brunette. Teaches kindergarten."

"Lauren?"

"Bingo."

David had never been sure what to make of Tina. Like tonight, though she was cordial, her eyes sparkled with an almost malevolent gleam. But the evening had been perfect and he wasn't going to let anything spoil it.

As soon as he could, David made some lame excuse about needing to take care of business and hurried over to Tom.

"I'm glad you could come tonight." David shook Tom's hand. "I hope you've been having a good time?"

"It's been unbelievable." Tom lowered his voice to a conspiratorial whisper. "That secretary of yours is one good-looking woman."

"You're not talking about Joni Thompson?" David couldn't hide his surprise. "Short brown hair? Blue eyes?"

"Don't look so shocked," Tom said. "She looks like a million bucks."

Obviously taking off those few hours must have been extremely productive ones for Joni. Although his administrative assistant was above average in looks, the level of admiration in Tom's voice was usually reserved for supermodels or beauty queens.

"I guess I hadn't noticed," David said.

Tom chuckled. "You're excused. You've barely taken your eyes off your wife the whole night."

David's gaze slid across the room. He found Christy standing by the dessert table talking to Sara and her husband.

"She is so beautiful." David's heart rose to his throat.

Tom turned to look and his gaze narrowed. "Sara Michaels? Yeah, she is hot, no doubt about it."

"Sara?" David shot Tom a disbelieving look. "I was talking about Christy."

Tom laughed and clapped David on the back. "Just kidding. You know what I think of Christy. She's the best."

David's gaze shifted back to Christy. He marveled at the way she interacted not only with Sara and Sal, but with the employees who stopped to speak to her.

"Look at her. She's such a natural," David said. "No wonder she's so successful."

"She makes everyone feel important," Tom said. "And that is a large part of her success. Speaking of which, what do you think about our girl going international? She's really hitting the big time now."

"International?" David kept his voice expressionless and tried not to show his surprise. "What do you mean?"

"Didn't she tell you?" Tom raised a brow.

"Sure she did," David said. "But I was busy with something else at the time and I guess I didn't pay close enough attention. So—" he brushed a piece of lint from his sleeve "—how many dates are you looking at?"

"Between the ones in the States and the ones in Europe, I can keep her busy almost continuously."

"Define almost continuously." A sick feeling filled the pit of David's stomach.

Tom paused and thought for a moment. "Two hundred plus days."

David stared disbelieving at Tom. "She'd be gone two thirds of the year. I can't believe Christy would agree to that."

"Well, it's true she hasn't signed the contracts yet," Tom said.

David breathed a sigh of relief.

"Though I have to tell you she *was* excited about the schedule," Tom continued.

"She was?" David didn't try to keep the skepticism from his tone.

"Yes, indeed." Tom's voice rang with a conviction that David found hard to question. "I know the woman, David. I know what her career means to her. She'll sign those contracts."

David wanted to tell Tom that he didn't know Christy as well as he thought he did. There would be no way Christy would go off to Europe. She'd promised to scale down her travel, not increase it.

"I guess we'll have to see," David said. There was no need to argue with Tom over the issue. Soon enough, Christy's publicist would discover for himself that though her career was important, it was no longer the top priority in Christy's life.

Tom smiled. "Yes, we will."

When Joni came by a few minutes later and whisked Tom out on the dance floor, David was relieved. He leaned against the wall.

Two hundred plus days.

"You look like you just lost your best friend." Sara's unexpected voice sounded soft and low against his ear.

David's lips automatically curved in a smile as he turned. Sara was dressed in a silver dress that hugged her every curve, and David had to agree with Tom that she was one beautiful woman. But David knew she was much more than a gorgeous shell. On the inside, she was just as beautiful.

"I want to thank you again for agreeing to sing on such short notice," David said.

"I appreciate being invited," Sara said. "Plus I owe you. My manager is convinced that *Entertain-*

ment Today interview really helped my latest album sales.''

David racked his brain trying to figure out what interview she might be referring to. ''You're not talking about that time at your house?''

''That's the one.'' Sara took a glass of champagne from a passing waiter. ''The publicity came at just the right time.''

''But I didn't have anything to do with it.''

''Sure you did,'' Sara said. ''I mean, Christy did. Her publicist and I talked earlier and he let it slip that he'd put a bug in their ear suggesting the taping.''

''So that's why she came back early.'' The anguish in David's voice nowhere near matched the disappointment in his soul. Why had Christy let him believe that she'd come back early for *him?* ''Not for your party or because she wanted to see me, but because of a chance for publicity.''

''It wasn't like that at all,'' Sara said. ''She hadn't realized the party was for her and…''

Sara rattled on, but David tuned her out.

His heart sank in his chest. All these months Christy had let him believe she'd come back for him. If she hadn't been honest about this, what else could she have lied about?

Christy leaned against the side of the bathroom stall partition. She drew a shaky breath and brushed a strand of hair back from her face with a trembling hand.

Thankfully the ladies' room had been empty when she'd made her mad dash, the crab puffs she'd eaten earlier pushing at the back of her throat.

What is wrong with me?

The stress of not knowing what was behind her myriad of strange symptoms had led her to make a doctor's appointment for early next week. But she'd felt so good the past couple of days, she'd been tempted to pick up the phone and cancel it. Now she was glad she hadn't.

Christy reached down and unraveled some toilet tissue, breaking off a couple of squares to wipe her mouth just as the door to the bathroom creaked open.

"Do you think it's true?" A feminine voice Christy didn't recognize spoke.

"I don't know, but the guy is my boss." The other female voice sounded vaguely familiar. "I could get fired for talking about him."

"Joni, chill out. We're the only ones in here," the first woman answered. "There's more chance we'll be overheard talking in the ballroom than in here."

Christy stood perfectly still. Obviously they

didn't realize she was in the handicapped stall tucked around the corner. If she were going to reveal herself, now would be the time. But would that be the best move? She would bet that the second voice, the one the other referred to as Joni, was David's administrative assistant. Though she didn't know the young woman very well, she seemed the sensitive sort. If Christy announced her presence at this point, it would probably ruin the young woman's evening.

Christy decided to remain silent and pray they didn't say anything she shouldn't hear.

"Okay," Joni said. "You're probably right."

"So, tell me. Do you think it's true?" The other woman's voice resonated with eager anticipation. "Has David Warner really been having an affair with his former girlfriend?"

Christy's breath caught in her throat and her heart pounded so loudly she was sure they could hear.

"Don't ask me," Joni said. "It's not like he confides the intimate details of his personal life to me."

"Yeah, but you're there with him every day," the other responded, clearly not interested in letting the subject drop. "Have you seen the old girlfriend around?"

''Lauren?'' Joni paused. ''Actually they went out for lunch together yesterday.''

Lauren? Everyone thought David was having an affair with Lauren? Christy's knees went weak with relief.

It never ceased to amaze her how people could make something out of nothing. She wished she could march out of the stall right then and tell the two women that David and Lauren had been friends for years. And that if they went to lunch together it was strictly *as* friends.

''That must have been when she told him about the baby,'' the first woman said, as if the pieces finally made sense. ''What do you think he'll do now?''

Baby? Christy frowned. What were they talking about?

''What *can* he do?'' Joni said with a sigh. ''Even if Lauren *is* having his baby, that doesn't change the fact that he's already married.''

Lauren was having David's baby? Every muscle in Christy's body tensed.

''What's her name?''

''His wife?'' Joni paused. ''It's Christy. She seems pretty nice, but I don't know her that well.''

''Didn't I hear he was drunk when he married her in Las Vegas?''

Christy's eyes filled with tears and she put her fist to her mouth.

"That's what everyone says," Joni said. "But I can't imagine Mr. Warner doing something like that. You should see how his face lights up when he talks about his wife...."

The voices faded until the door closed, leaving Christy once again alone.

She took a deep breath and wiped the tears from her face with the back of her hand. Exiting the stall, she hurried to the mirror and tried not to think about what the women had said. Instead she pressed a cold paper towel to her face and fought the bile rising in her throat.

It took all her inner strength to maintain some semblance of control. She took deep breaths until she was convinced that she could walk back out into the ballroom without losing control.

She hadn't gone more than a few steps when she ran into David's grandfather.

"Why, Christy, my dear," he said with a warm smile. "Don't you look lovely tonight."

"Thank you. You're looking pretty dapper yourself." Christy's voice came out steady and smooth and she said a little prayer of thanks. "Say, have you seen Lauren? I needed to speak to her about something, but our paths haven't crossed lately."

"You're in luck," David's grandfather said. "I

just saw her a few minutes ago. She was over by the punch bowl talking to Sara Michaels.''

''I'd better go catch her quick.'' She flashed David's grandfather a smile and headed straight for the punch bowl.

If Lauren was pregnant with David's baby, she needed to know. Unfortunately Christy wasn't sure what she was going to do if the gossip were true.

At this moment, she could only pray to God it wasn't.

Chapter Seventeen

"Lauren, can I speak with you a minute?" Christy didn't even try to fake a smile. "It's important."

"But Sara and I..." Lauren's voice trailed off.

"I need to see what my husband is up to, anyway," Sara said quickly. "I'll see you both later."

"That was kind of rude, don't you think?" Lauren said.

"At this moment I don't really care." Christy paused and gathered her courage. "Are you going to have a baby?"

Lauren's eyes widened. She took a step back. "He told you, didn't he?"

Christy's heart quivered. "David's my husband. Don't you think I have a right to know?"

"No, I don't." To Christy's surprise Lauren looked more angry than embarrassed. "I specifically told him not to say anything to anyone yet."

Christy took a deep breath and tried to keep her tone matter-of-fact. "Why the secrecy? In time everyone will know, anyway."

"Not if I don't go through with it," Lauren said. "I'm having second thoughts. I'd be alone. It wouldn't be easy."

Christy gasped in horror. She couldn't believe Lauren would consider such a step. She grasped for anything to stop this madness. "But you've always wanted a child. We used to talk about what it would be like to have a baby of our own some day. Remember?"

"Yes, but if you recall, those dreams always included a husband. And the man I'd always wanted at my side is now yours." A sadness filled Lauren's gaze. "Anyway, it's my body. My decision. My life. And I really don't want to talk about this with you."

Lauren turned to go, but stopped and shifted her gaze back to Christy for a moment. "Tell David thanks a lot. I thought I could count on him to keep this to himself. Obviously I was wrong."

In an instant she was gone and Christy collapsed into a nearby chair, her heart pounding.

Would Lauren really consider terminating her

pregnancy just because she didn't want to go through it alone? Didn't she realize there were individuals and agencies more than willing to help her every step of the way?

The woman she'd known all those years ago wouldn't have considered taking such a step, but then that Lauren would never have had an affair with a married man.

Unless he wasn't married when she'd slept with him.

When they'd said their vows, David had surprised her by already having an engagement ring in his pocket. Christy buried her face in her hands. If she'd never bumped into David in Las Vegas, he'd be married to Lauren by now and she'd be thinking about baby showers, not the unthinkable.

What Christy couldn't figure out was why David hadn't told her. He had to know she'd find out. Was it because he thought it wouldn't matter anyway, knowing how Christy felt about divorce?

She couldn't presume to know what he was thinking. But Christy did know there was only one solution. David needed to be free to marry Lauren and raise their child. If he couldn't leave her, she would just have to leave him.

If one more person stopped and asked her if she was having fun, Christy was going to scream.

So far she'd managed to keep a smile on her face and make polite if uninspiring conversation. But her tightly held control was starting to unravel.

She needed to be alone so she could gather her thoughts and regroup. But where could she go? The rest room certainly held no appeal. And even if she took a seat at an empty table, she could almost guarantee she wouldn't be by herself for long.

Christy thought for a moment. Hadn't someone told her this hotel had a beautiful veranda?

"Would you like a glass of champagne?" A baby-faced waiter held out a silver tray.

Christy shook her head and smiled a polite refusal.

The waiter turned to go, but he hadn't gone more than a few steps when Christy stopped him.

"Wait."

The young man spun on his heel. "Change your mind?"

"Actually I wanted to ask you something," she said. "I'd like to get some fresh air. Someone mentioned a veranda?"

"Yes, ma'am." He gestured to a set of French doors at the far end of the ballroom. "It's right out those doors."

"Thank you."

"Sure you wouldn't like to take a glass with you?" he said with an enticing smile.

Christy shook her head. "I think I'll pass."

Her head was muddled enough right now. She certainly didn't need to add alcohol to the equation.

As she made her way across the ballroom, she caught a glimpse of David surrounded by a group of men. He lifted a hand in greeting and Christy managed a weak smile.

Thank goodness he was occupied, or he'd probably come looking for her. And she wasn't ready to talk to him. Not yet, anyway.

Feeling like a spy in a low-budget movie, Christy glanced around to make sure no one was looking, then pushed open the French doors and slipped out of the stuffy ballroom into the cool night air. The glow from strategically placed lights gave the open area an oddly intimate atmosphere.

Christy moved to the railing. There was so much to think about, so much to consider.

"What's up?" a deep voice rumbled in her ear.

Christy whirled around, her heart pounding in her chest. She recognized him instantly. Her breath came out in a whoosh and she sagged against the rail. "Rusty, you scared me to death. What are you doing out here?"

She quickly scanned the veranda, expecting to see Lauren. The other woman was nowhere in sight. If tonight was his big chance to get Lauren's attention, why wasn't he with her now?

Unless he knows about the baby, she thought.

Her gaze returned to Rusty, but he'd moved past her to the railing and stood staring out into the darkness. She hesitated, sensing his sadness.

"Are you okay?" Christy tentatively touched his arm.

He shrugged, but she already knew the answer. She could see it in the slump of his shoulders and the way his lips drooped like a dejected child.

"Things rocky between you and Lauren?" Christy felt bad about pushing him when it was obvious he didn't want to talk. But she consoled herself with the knowledge that if he *really* didn't want to talk he shouldn't have approached her in the first place. And, for the moment, focusing on his problems kept her from thinking about her own.

"You could say so." Rusty took so long to answer Christy had almost forgotten the question. But when his voice cracked and he paused to swipe a hand across his eyes, her heart went out to him.

"She told me tonight that there can never be anything more between us than just friendship." The imploring eyes he turned to Christy were filled with pain and confusion. "Why would she say that? We'd been having such a good time. I don't understand."

Christy had her own theory of why, but she kept silent. It certainly wasn't her place to tell Rusty about Lauren's baby. He'd find out soon enough on his own.

"Sometimes it's hard to know why things happen the way they do," Christy said, thinking of her own relationship with David. "I guess we have to trust in God that it will all work out in the end."

"But Lauren and I are perfect together," he said.

"That might be," Christy said. "You can't make someone love you. If Lauren doesn't have those feelings for you, she just doesn't."

"You make it sound simple. It's not," Rusty said. "I've been in love with Lauren since I was fifteen."

Christy thought back to those dark days of senior year when David had walked out of her life.

"Oh, Rusty, I know it's not simple or easy," she said softly. "When David and I broke up in high school, I didn't think I could go on. I loved him so much and I couldn't understand why he didn't feel the same. I wanted to plead with him to stay with me. But I couldn't do it. I had too much pride."

Rusty's gaze met hers. "So what did you do?"

"I told myself that if David and I were meant to be together, it would happen." Christy hesitated.

She'd never talked about this so frankly with anyone before. But she hoped Rusty would find some comfort in her words. "Now I realize that if he hadn't broken up with me, I probably wouldn't have gone to Princeton. I guess what I'm trying to say is because of that decision, my life took a different turn. Maybe because of Lauren's decision, your life will go in a different direction. Maybe you're destined to meet someone else you wouldn't have met if you and Lauren were still involved. Or maybe down the road you'll be able to help a friend in a similar situation because you'll understand what he's going through."

"I wouldn't wish this on a friend," Rusty said.

Christy silently agreed. Her marriage and impending divorce might make her a better therapist and educator, but she would give anything not to have had her life turn out this way. "I wouldn't either."

Her gaze met his and they shared a smile of understanding.

"You know, I never liked you," he said.

The sentiment didn't surprise her. "I know," she said. "I never understood why."

"This might not make any sense," Rusty said. "But it was because David liked you and not Lauren."

"You're right," Christy said, shaking her head.

"That doesn't make sense. I would have thought you'd have been thrilled she and David weren't together."

"The problem was I always wanted Lauren to be happy," he said. "She wanted David in the worst way and you were the only thing standing between them."

Christy wanted to point out that after she'd left town, David and Lauren could have connected, but she kept silent.

"It's odd, isn't it?" she said simply. "How everyone always seems to want what they can't have."

"But it worked out for you. You and David ended up together," Rusty said.

Yes, but for how much longer?

"You're a good guy, Rusty," Christy said softly. "One of these days you'll find someone who'll return your love."

"Do you really think so?"

Christy nodded.

Rusty stared at her for a long moment. "You know, I can see why David married you."

"Thank you," Christy said. "That means a lot."

"Maybe when I get a new girlfriend, the four of us can go out sometime."

It was amazing. Rusty's broken heart had already started to mend.

Though she prayed hers would heal as quickly, Christy had her doubts. Leaving David would be the hardest thing she'd ever have to do. But in the end, what choice did she have?

Lauren's baby deserved a chance at life, and Christy was going to see that it got that chance.

David had been uncharacteristically silent during the drive home, so Christy hadn't had to worry about making small talk. But the moment they walked through the front door, that changed. His gaze met hers and when he said he'd make some hot chocolate and then they could talk, her heart clenched.

A few minutes later she leaned back in the kitchen chair and swirled a marshmallow in her cup with the tip of her finger. "What do you want to talk about?"

"I think you know."

Had he finally decided to tell her the truth? A part of her hoped he would. The part that wanted to believe if they were open and honest they could find a solution. Lauren needed David. And Christy had to make sure that nothing, and no one, stood between them.

She slowly licked the sticky sweetness from her fingertip. "I don't think I do."

David's jaw tightened, but it wasn't anger that

filled his eyes but something else. "Let's start with the reason you came to Sara's party."

"What are you talking about?" Christy's voice reflected her surprise.

"I'm talking about Sara's party in March," he said with exaggerated patience. "Why did you come?"

"Because you asked me to come?" Christy said. What in the world did this have to do with Lauren?

"You came—" David spoke slowly, emphasizing each word "—because you wanted the publicity."

"I wanted to be with you," she said.

He raked his fingers through his hair and exhaled a harsh breath. "C'mon, Christy. Just say it. You came because you knew *Entertainment Today* would be there."

"Okay, maybe I did come initially because of that, but—"

David waved her silent. "You lied to me, Christy. What I can't understand is why."

Christy shifted her gaze to the cocoa and stifled the desire to defend herself. Though it was hard to bear the disappointment in his eyes, she had to let him believe the worst. She had to keep silent.

After she'd spoken with Lauren, Christy had worried that when she told David she was leaving him he wouldn't let her go. Or he'd try to convince her to stay and she'd weaken and give in. If she played this right, he'd want her to go.

"Tom said you'd be traveling a lot next year," he said, surprising her by changing the subject.

"Yeah, isn't that great?" Christy forced some enthusiasm into her words. "If I want to, I can do more seminars next year than I've done in the last two years combined."

It was a frightening thought, but the truth.

"And do you want to?" David's voice was low and strained.

"Sure." Christy deliberately lifted one shoulder in a casual shrug. "I know I talked about cutting back, but Tom has convinced me that I need to travel to hit the big time. The way I look at it, I don't have a choice. At this point, my career has to come first."

"I thought you were different." David spoke so softly that his words were but a whisper.

Though the resignation and disappointment in his tone tore at Christy's heartstrings, she reminded herself that a baby's life was at stake. Compared to that, nothing else mattered.

She held her breath and waited for him to say that if that's the way she felt, their marriage was over.

He drew a long, shuddering breath. "If that's the way you feel, I guess..."

Christy braced herself.

"...we'll just have to find a way to make it work."

Christy's eyes widened. Her heart gave an absurd little leap. He really did love her. *Dear God, why now?* His willingness to compromise only complicated matters.

"I don't think you understand." It took everything Christy had to keep her voice steady. "I had some surveys done, and a divorce won't affect my career as much as I first thought. And this is a good time for me to make those changes. I realize it might not be as good for you, but if your grandfather gives you any trouble, blame it all on me."

"Are you saying you want a divorce?" His face blanched.

Christy swallowed hard, forced a smile and nodded. "That's what I'm saying."

"I love you, Christy," David said.

Christy wanted to tell him she loved him, too. She wanted to pull him to her and feel his strong arms wrapped around her. She wanted to tell David that the only place she wanted to be was by his side.

Instead, she bit her tongue and thought of that innocent little baby.

"I'm sorry, David." She rose to her feet. "It really is best if we end it now."

"But Christy—"

"Like I said, I'm sorry." She paused. "We never were right for each other. It would have been better if you'd married Lauren, like you'd planned."

"I don't want Lauren," he roared.

She ignored him and headed up the stairs, praying to God that with her out of the picture he *would* want Lauren. *And* her baby.

Chapter Eighteen

David shoved the papers on his desk to the side with a sweep of his arm. He didn't care about reports or proposals.

Why had she left him?

Sure, he might have been a little angry about her lying to him, but was that a reason to call it quits? He'd thought she was committed to making their marriage work.

He heaved a resigned sigh and leaned back in the chair. His thoughts drifted back to all that had happened since Las Vegas.

Initially he'd been the one who'd wanted out. At least, that's what he'd said. But deep down he had to admit that from the time he'd been seventeen, Christy had been the only woman he'd ever wanted. Now she was gone.

And David wished to God he knew why.

* * *

Diplomas and awards lined the walls of the doctor's office. Christy read each one thoroughly while she waited for Dr. James to come in and tell her what was wrong.

The doctor had listened carefully as she'd detailed the various symptoms that had been plaguing her for months. As she'd talked, she'd watched carefully for any reaction. Was that a frown when she'd mentioned the overwhelming fatigue that had only recently started to lessen? And was it only her imagination or did his pen pause when she'd talked about having an appetite that would put a truck driver to shame?

At the end of her litany, he'd only said in that no-nonsense voice of his that it was definitely something that needed to be checked out. A nurse had come in and drawn some blood before sending her to a tiny bathroom for a urine sample.

Once that had been accomplished, Christy had been shown to a lavender exam room filled with posters about Breast Self Exam and Preventing Sexually Transmitted Diseases and had been told the doctor would be in to do an exam.

He didn't seem to be much of a talker, but she desperately wanted to know what he was thinking. At the end of the exam, he'd finally spoken, but not to her. Turning to the nurse, he'd grunted something about setting up a time for an ultrasound.

Christy's blood ran cold. When she'd lived in Chicago, a neighbor had been fighting a losing battle with ovarian cancer. Christy was almost sure that Brenda had said an ultrasound was one of the first tests they'd done when they were trying to find a diagnosis. Now Dr. James wanted her to have one?

Christy had tried to press him to tell her what he thought was wrong, but he'd just asked her to get dressed and told her they'd talk in his office.

Now here she was, waiting again. Never had she needed David more. Christy dabbed at her eyes with a tissue. She wished he could be beside her now, flashing that smile of his and putting his arm around her, calling her Chrissy and telling her everything was going to be fine. Telling her that she wasn't alone because they were in this together.

But she *was* alone. A tear traveled down her cheek. She'd made sure of that. Since she'd walked out on David, she'd refused to return his phone calls or to see him. What choice did she have? Lauren's baby's life hung in the balance. This wasn't about her love for David—it was about the greater good.

And anyway, she reminded herself, she wasn't

really alone. God would always be beside her every step of the way.

"Mrs. Warner, I've got a diagnosis for you." Dr. James strolled into the office, shook her hand and took a seat behind the massive cherry-wood desk. "The urine test confirms my physical findings."

"You already know what's wrong with me?" Christy sank into a nearby chair, her knees like jelly.

"Indeed I do." His gaze turned sharp and assessing. "I was hoping your husband would be here with you."

This was her opportunity to let the doctor know that she was on her own, that she and David were no longer together. But the words wouldn't come. She swallowed hard and knew God would forgive her this tiny lie. "David wanted to come. But he had a meeting and couldn't get away."

"That's too bad." Dr. James took off his half glasses and slipped them into the pocket of his lab coat. "I usually enjoy giving this kind of news to both of you."

"Enjoy?" Christy tried to stem the well of hope that rose at the unexpected word. "This is good news?"

"I certainly think so." Dr. James smiled.

"There's nothing wrong with you, Mrs. Warner. Nothing that five more months won't cure."

She puzzled over his words before realization dawned. "Are you saying I'm pregnant?"

Dr. James nodded, a broad smile blanketing his face.

"But how can that be?" she blurted out. "My doctor in Chicago told me with my endometriosis I'd have a hard time getting pregnant."

"Apparently he was wrong." The doctor chuckled.

"But what about the ultrasound?" she said. "I heard you tell the nurse she needed to schedule one."

"To confirm how far along you are," he said.

"A baby?" Too shocked to even think clearly, Christy's hand dropped protectively to her abdomen. "I'm really going to have a baby?"

"Right about Thanksgiving time is my guess," he said. "The ultrasound should confirm that. I'll start you on prenatal vitamins and we'll want you to…"

Christy barely heard what he said. All she could think of was that David's and her child would be born at Thanksgiving…just in time for their divorce.

David waited until two to take his lunch break, hoping that the small park close to his office would be deserted.

The crowd that filled the green wooden benches over the noon hour should be back at work, so he'd have the entire place to himself. Which was good, since the last thing David felt like doing was making small talk.

In fact, he hadn't felt like doing much of anything since Christy had moved into a hotel. It had been less than a week, but it seemed like forever. He missed running with her in the morning, talking with her on the phone in between meetings and seeing her smiling face when he came home from work. But the nights were the hardest. They'd been married four months and he'd grown so used to having her beside him. He'd loved lying next to her and breathing in the scent of her perfume while her warm body curved against his.

We were so good together.

He angrily brushed some moisture from his eyes and tried to still the hurt that encircled his heart like a noose.

"David. Joni said I might find you here."

David jerked his gaze up to find Lauren standing before him. He blinked twice and resisted the urge to wipe his eyes with the back of his hand. "What's up?"

She gestured to the bench. "Do you mind if I

sit down for a minute? I don't mean to interrupt, but I really need to talk to you about something.''

''Sure.'' David scooted over to make more room for her. ''Have a seat.''

Lauren sat down and David could tell by the two lines of worry between her brows that something was bothering her.

''I was talking to Sara yesterday and she told me there was a disturbing rumor going around at the party.''

The first thought that popped into David's mind was that the word must be out that he and Christy were separating. But then David realized that Christy hadn't walked out on him until *after* the party. Actually things had been good between them until that point.

''David?'' Lauren's eyes narrowed. ''Are you listening to me?''

''I'm sorry.'' He offered her an apologetic smile and his full attention. ''My mind wandered for a minute. What were you saying?''

''I asked how Christy was doing?''

David's heart clenched. Though he and Lauren had been friends for years, David couldn't bring himself to tell her the truth. He knew it was because he still hadn't given up hope that he and Christy would reconcile. ''Christy is fine. Busy.''

Lauren gave a long audible sigh. "I'm glad. I was so afraid that—"

"You were afraid what?" David said when she didn't continue.

"There were some horrible rumors going around at the party. I was worried Christy might have heard them and—" Lauren hesitated and gave a helpless shrug "—believed them."

David met her gaze. "What kind of rumors are we talking about?"

"I guess I might as well tell you." A flush traveled up Lauren's neck. "They were saying I was pregnant with your baby."

"Pregnant!" David sat upright. "We never even—"

"I know that," Lauren said. "But apparently whoever started this story didn't know that or didn't care."

"But where would someone have ever gotten such a crazy idea in the first place?"

"I can't say for sure," Lauren said. "Although I have my suspicions."

"And that is?"

"Remember when we were in Conroy's and I told you I was thinking about having a baby by artificial insemination?" She paused. "You told me a baby needs both parents and I really needed to think long and hard about this decision?"

"Of course I remember," David said. "But what does that have to do with anything?"

"Did you tell Christy about my plans?"

"Not a word," he said. "You told me not to say anything."

"I was afraid of that." Lauren leaned back against the bench and exhaled a deep breath.

"Lauren, don't leave me hanging here," David said. "Tell me what's going on."

"Okay," she said. "But you're not going to like it."

"Just tell me."

"Christy approached me at the party. From the way she was talking I got the impression you'd told her about my plans," she said. "But when Sara came to me about the rumors I realized that maybe that's what Christy was really asking me about. And thinking back on my answers, I realized she might have gotten a totally wrong impression."

"And what impression would that be?"

"That I *was* pregnant with your baby," Lauren said in a rush. "And that I was thinking of having an abortion, since I didn't want to raise a child alone."

"But how would she get that idea?" David frowned. "What did you say to her?"

"We just talked. She asked me a lot of questions, but I thought she was referring to the artificial insemination, and then when Sara told me what people were saying, I thought she…" Lauren waved a dismissive hand. "Since she's not upset, that obviously wasn't the impression she got. But I've been worried about it since yesterday when I talked to Sara, and I just had to make sure that everything was okay between you two."

"Everything is fine," David said firmly. And it was. Now he knew why Christy had walked out on him. Now he just had to find her and get this whole mess straightened out.

Chapter Nineteen

Christy couldn't help it. She knew she shouldn't put herself through such torture by going to a place that held memories of David, but she needed to think and to pray.

The hotel room where she'd spent the past three nights held no appeal. But the tiny park close to Warner Enterprises where she and David had often met for lunch was strangely appealing. It was after two-thirty and the lunch crowd would be long gone. There was no chance she'd run into David, since he always preferred to take an early lunch and keep his afternoons free for meetings.

The parking lot next to the park was deserted except for a new Saturn parked at the far end. Christy shut off the car and reached for the turkey sandwich and carton of milk she'd picked up at the deli after she'd left the doctor's office. Dr. James had told her it was best for her baby if she ate regular nutritious meals.

Christy's gaze fell and she lightly stroked her abdomen through her cotton dress.

A baby.

She wanted to laugh and cry all at the same time. A week ago she would have been ecstatic. Now the news only brought up more questions. More decisions.

When should she tell David? If she told him now, he might refuse to give her a divorce. A chill traveled up her spine at the thought of what would happen to Lauren and her baby if that occurred.

Unlike Lauren, Christy would never consider terminating her pregnancy. If she had to raise this baby alone, she would. She was grateful she'd already told Tom she was going to cut back on her travel next year and that the contracts she'd signed were mostly in the Midwest.

Tom had warned her that such a decision could seriously impact her career, but Christy knew she'd made the right decision. Despite what Tom thought, she didn't want to spend the next few years of her life in an airplane. She'd wanted to stay close to home and to David.

It would have been wonderful if things had been

different. If she could have been hurrying through this gilt-edged gate to tell David he was going to be a father.

Christy wiped the sudden tears away with the back of her hand and headed down the sidewalk. If she'd been paying closer attention, she might have heard the footsteps. Instead, deep in thought, she followed the walk as it curved to the left and bumped smack into a firm, broad chest.

"I'm so sorr—" Her head jerked up and her breath caught in her throat. "David."

"Chrissy." He breathed her name and for an instant the look in his eyes turned her insides to mush.

"I'd better get going."

The familiar feminine voice pulled Christy back to reality with a crash. Her gaze shifted to her husband's companion.

Lauren.

Heat rose in her cheeks as if she'd been slapped. It was what she'd wanted, but when she met David's gaze she couldn't keep the hurt from her eyes. A pain sharp as any knife sliced her heart.

"I'm sorry." Lauren brushed past Christy and took off down the sidewalk as if a dog was nipping at her heels.

"Christy, let me explain...." David took her arm.

"Don't touch me!" She pulled from his grasp, her breath coming in short puffs. Her lunch sack dropped unnoticed to the ground. The sobs were rising in her chest and she knew if she didn't get away soon, she'd end up falling apart.

She turned on her heel and started down the same path Lauren had disappeared down only a moment before. Christy had gone only a few steps before David caught her. But this time he wouldn't let go.

"Listen to me." David's hazel eyes flashed. "Lauren was just telling me that—"

"It's not my business anymore." Christy averted her gaze. "You don't need to explain anything to me."

"I think I do," he said softly.

She couldn't help it. Christy turned her head and met his gaze. "Maybe I don't want to hear it."

"Lauren's not pregnant."

"Oh, no." Christy's hand rose to her throat. "She didn't have—"

"She's never been pregnant."

"Don't lie to me, David," Christy said softly, narrowing her gaze. "She told me herself—"

"She'd told me she was going to have a baby by artificial insemination," David said. "That's what she thought you were talking about."

She couldn't help it. A tiny shred of hope rose

inside her. But no matter how much Christy wanted to believe him, the evidence was just too overwhelming.

"But the women in the rest room said she was pregnant with your baby." Despite her resolve not to cry, a few tears slipped past her lids and ran down her cheeks.

"I don't care what they said," David replied. "It's not true."

"How can you be so sure?"

"Because I've never made love to Lauren," he said, wiping her tears away with his fingers. "Since I've been seventeen, there's only been one woman for me."

Christy swallowed hard against the sudden lump in her throat.

"I've never loved anyone but you." His gaze met hers and the depth of emotion in his eyes took her breath away. He took a step closer, reaching up with one hand to push a strand of hair gently back from her face as he brushed her lips with his own.

Christy wasn't sure who made the next move, but it took just a fraction of a second for her to fall into his arms. He kissed her again, longer this time, letting his mouth linger. It was still as sweet, though, still as gentle.

"And when the time comes," he said softly,

"there's only one woman I want to have my babies."

A comforting warmth filled her body and Christy couldn't keep the smile from her lips. "Is Thanksgiving too soon for you?"

"Thanksgiving?" David said with a puzzled frown.

"You said when the time comes—" her grin widened "—and I'm saying Thanksgiving is going to be that time."

"We're going to have a baby?" The words tumbled from his lips.

Christy nodded.

"Praise the Lord." David let out a whoop and twirled her around.

Christy could only laugh.

Praise the Lord, indeed.

Epilogue

❧

Valentine's Day
Two years later

Christy lit the crimson candles on the dining-room table and stepped back, admiring the way the glow reflected off the crystal goblets. It was hard to believe that tonight she and David would celebrate their second anniversary. A shiver of excitement traveled up her spine. He'd told her he had a surprise for her. She'd laughed and told him that they were even then, because she had a surprise for him, too.

She untied her apron and placed it carefully in the drawer, taking out the CD she'd hidden there earlier. Her lips curved in satisfaction as she slid the disc into the player and one of the "world's greatest love songs" filled the room.

Everything was ready.

She didn't have to worry about Max. Tom and Joni had offered to keep the toddler overnight. With a new baby of their own in the house, they'd told her their Valentine's Day celebration was definitely going to be a family one, and the little boy was more than welcome.

Christy wanted the dinner to be perfect. Actually, she wanted the night to be perfect. She'd changed both the dinner menu and her outfit several times before settling on lobster Newburg and a clingy black dress she'd bought a few months ago. Looking down at the jersey fabric, she still wondered if she shouldn't have gone with a larger size.

The doorbell interrupted her thoughts. Christy hurried to open the front door.

"Lauren, hello." Christy opened the door wide and gestured for her friend to come inside. "I love that red dress."

"Thank you, I picked it up on a pre-Valentine's Day sale. Speaking of which, I can only stay a few minutes." Lauren stepped inside. "A whole group of us are going out to dinner to celebrate V-Day. Rusty and Melanie are picking me up at seven and told me I have to be ready."

"So Rusty asked her out for Valentine's Day," Christy said. "Sounds like it's getting serious."

"I think you're right," Lauren said. "He's definitely got it bad. And she seems to feel the same. It's good to see him so happy."

"Love can do that to you." Christy thought of the joy her husband and son had brought into *her* life. "How's it going with you and Nate?"

Lauren shrugged. "He's fun to be with, but that's about it."

Christy touched her friend's arm. "One of these days you'll find that special someone."

"Maybe. I just hope he shows up before my biological clock stops ticking," Lauren said with a smile. "So I'll have someone besides my little godson to spoil rotten. Where is Max, anyway?"

"Over at Joni and Tom's for the evening," Christy said.

"Well, when you see him, give him this." Lauren pulled a red bear out of the sack she carried. "And tell him his aunt Lauren loves him to pieces."

"I will."

They chatted for a few minutes before Lauren took a look at the clock and squealed.

"Got to go." Lauren grabbed her purse and headed for the door.

Christy barely had a chance to say goodbye before Lauren drove off. Being able to get back on her old footing with Lauren had been only one of the many blessings that had come Christy's way in the past two years.

After Max was born she'd made her husband and son her primary focus. She'd cut back to one seminar a month and embarked on a career as a Christian counselor. And now she'd restricted her practice to two days a week.

David, too, had made changes. He'd worked out an arrangement with Blake to share the responsibilities for managing Warner Enterprises. This not only allowed both of them to use their God-given talents to the fullest but also gave David more time with his family.

The front door slammed and Christy's heart thumped in her chest. *Please God, let him be happy with the news.*

She barely had time to smooth her hair and wipe a fingerprint from a wineglass before David was in the room, standing behind her, the spicy scent of his cologne teasing her senses.

"How's my Valentine girl?" He gently massaged her shoulders.

"Happy." Christy smiled and turned in her husband's arms. "I was just standing here thinking how God has blessed me. I am so very lucky."

"You have a wonderful job—" His fingers played with her hair.

"—that gives me great satisfaction," she said, her voice slightly breathless.

"A handsome husband—" He lowered his head and nibbled at her ear.

"—whom I adore." Her heart hammered in her ears.

"And a son—" His lips traveled a path along her jawline.

"—who means the world to me." She turned her mouth to meet his.

David's eyes lit up and he brushed a kiss that was way too brief across her lips.

"Speaking of the world..." David reached into his suit coat and pulled out a travel folder. "I've got a Valentine's gift for you. What would you say to a couple of weeks in Belize? Sort of a belated honeymoon?"

Christy didn't need to close her eyes to picture it. Lying on the beach with David. The warm sand. The blue skies. The endless nights.

It had been her favorite dream when they'd first been married. But then the baby had come and...

"Who'd take care of Max?" she said, realizing suddenly that she hadn't even thought about her son.

"I've already cleared it with your parents. They

jumped at the chance," he said with a chuckle. "You know how they feel about spending time with their grandson."

"And they never can tell their son-in-law no," Christy said, realizing that her parents fully accepting David as part of the family was yet another blessing.

"Whatever the reason," he said with characteristic modesty, "it's a go. All you have to do is say when."

Christy didn't hesitate. "Next month?"

"That soon?" he said. "I mean, that would be great, but can you get your schedule freed up by then?"

"I'll have to," Christy said. "Because I want to still be able to wear a bikini. And if we wait too much longer, that's not going to happen."

"What difference would a few months make?" David's brows drew together for a long moment before the light of understanding replaced the confusion in his eyes. "You're pregnant?"

She nodded. "Are you pleased?"

"Oh, Chrissy." David pulled her close and kissed her slowly, lingeringly.

"So you're happy about the baby?" After Max was born, she and David had talked about more children, but she'd never expected it to happen this soon.

"I couldn't have asked for a better Valentine's Day gift."

A warmth of pleasure stole through her. "Really?"

He curled his finger beneath her chin and lifted her face to meet his gaze. "It's been two years since Las Vegas. I've never thought of myself as particularly lucky, but right now I feel like the luckiest man in the world."

David's lips lowered to hers before Christy could tell him it wasn't luck at all. Before she could tell him that God was the dealer in this game called love and with Him stacking the deck, a winning hand was always guaranteed.

*   *   *   *   *

Dear Reader,

In June of 1999 I sold my first book, *Unforgettable Faith*, to Steeple Hill's Love Inspired line. I can hardly believe it's been three years! *Wedding Bell Blues* is my sixth book for Love Inspired, and I feel truly blessed to have been given the continued opportunity to write these kinds of books. Writing inspirational romance allows me to combine my faith in God with my love of romance. As we know, with both God and romance, a happy ending is guaranteed.

I hope you enjoy this book. I love to hear from readers so I encourage you to visit my Web site http://www.cynthiarutledge.com and drop me a line!

All my best,

Cynthia Rutledge

Next Month From Steeple Hill®'s

Love Inspired
Change of the Heart
by
Lynn Bulock

When an accident landed Carrie Collins in the
emergency room, the feisty redhead didn't exactly
hit it off with the handsome—and bossy—
Dr. Rafe O'Connor. But when they were thrown
together during a church-sponsored mission trip, they
just might realize they were meant for each other!

**Don't miss
CHANGE OF THE HEART**

On sale August 2002

Take 2 inspirational love stories FREE!

PLUS get a FREE surprise gift!

Mail to Steeple Hill Reader Service™

In U.S.	**In Canada**
3010 Walden Ave.	P.O. Box 609
P.O. Box 1867	Fort Erie, Ontario
Buffalo, NY 14240-1867	L2A 5X3

YES! Please send me 2 free Love Inspired® novels and my free surprise gift. After receiving them, if I don't wish to receive anymore, I can return the shipping statement marked cancel. If I don't cancel, I will receive 3 brand-new novels every month, before they're available in stores! Bill me at the low price of $3.99 each in the U.S. and $4.49 each in Canada, plus 25¢ shipping and handling and applicable sales tax, if any*. That's the complete price and a saving of over 10% off the cover prices—quite a bargain! I understand that accepting the books and gift places me under no obligation ever to buy any books. I can always return a shipment and cancel at any time. Even if I never buy another book from Steeple Hill, the 2 free books and the surprise gift are mine to keep forever.

103 IDN DNU6
303 IDN DNU7

Name	(PLEASE PRINT)
Address	Apt. No.
City	State/Prov. Zip/Postal Code

Next Month From Steeple Hill®'s

Love Inspired®

Family for Keeps
by
Margaret Daley

Pediatric nurse Tess Morgan's dreams of having a large
family were shattered by a devastating tragedy. But just
when she'd lost all hope for the future, she was drawn
to a strong and tender single father who was no
stranger to grief. Together, could they discover the
healing power of God's love?

Don't miss
FAMILY FOR KEEPS

On sale August 2002

LIFFK

Next Month From Steeple Hill's

Love Inspired

Tucker's Bride
by
Lois Richer

After seven years away, the man who'd promised to
marry Ginny Brown was back in Jubilee Junction.
Deep in her soul, Ginny knew God intended them to
build a life together. But would it take a miracle to
recapture Tucker's disillusioned heart—and
restore his lost faith?

Don't miss
TUCKER'S BRIDE

On sale August 2002